PARALLELS

Vũ Đình Giang (b. 1976) is from the Mekong delta. He has published several novels and short stories. He studied applied arts at Ho Chi Minh City University of Architecture and currently lives and works in Ho Chi Minh City as visual art editor at Kim Đồng Publishing House. Originally published in Vietnamese in 2007, and translated into French in 2014, *Parallels* is his first novel.

Khải Q. Nguyễn's writings appear in literary journals in Chile, Indonesia, Nigeria, Singapore, and Venezuela. His English translations of Vietnamese novels published by Major Books include *Parallels* (2025), and *The Young Die Old* (2026). He has master's degrees in comparative literature and cultural studies from the universities of Perpignan, St Andrews, and Santiago de Compostela.

PRAISES

'*Parallels* is a Wong Kar-wai movie of a novel: stylish and cool, erotic and yet touched with violence. An iconic work of Vietnamese queer literature now set to be embraced by the world.'

–Anton Hur, Korean writer & translator, author of *Toward Eternity*

'Reading through Vũ Đình Giang's *Parallels*, translated by Khai Q. Nguyen, is like treading through a strange swamp. The book fearlessly obscures itself with its use of the epistolary forms, but it also charms us with the subtle narrative threads connecting the lives of its characters. The characters also resist formula: they are cryptic and erudite, cultured and self-sabotaging, complex and humane.'

–Norman Erikson Pasaribu, author & poet of *My Dream Job*

'I did not know the work by Vũ Đình Giang before. When I read it, I appreciated his innovations and audacious writing style. I was struck by the darkness of the text. I had the impression that I had in my hand what is called a "literary UFO." A strong and beautiful text. And I told myself that I absolutely had to translate it.'

–Yves Bouillé, French translator of *Parallels*

Major Books Ltd, 128 City Road, London, United Kingdom, EC1V 2NX
First published in the United Kingdom in 2025 by Major Books

Originally published in Vietnamese as *Song Song* in 2007
by Văn Nghệ publishing house

Edited by Samuel Tan

A CIP catalogue record for this book is available from the British Library
ISBN 978-1-917233-06-4
eISBN 978-1-917233-07-1

Typeset in Garamond Premier Pro by Coral Books JSC
Printed and bound in Vietnam by Hai Phong Stationery Joint Stock Company

www.major-books.com

Vũ Đình Giang

PARALLELS

Translated by KHẢI Q. NGUYỄN

MAJOR BOOKS

TABLE OF CONTENTS

03 Bio

04 Praises

11 Content

275 Afterword

As the sun disappears, I come into life...

G.g

That's my signature, which sometimes creates misunderstandings and causes a lot of trouble. A bright name is certainly more pleasant, but not for me, because I belong to the darker realms. Symbols often carry more mysterious layers of meaning. It suits me. So call me G.g.

I am H.

I lead a life of loneliness. I can sleep with many different people, and know how to accept the end of short-lived relationships; I barely know the meaning of hurt. In essence, I am emotionless.

I discovered that I could hardly get rid of G.g. Since then, I have almost been unable to bear the feeling of attachment. I've struggled to get out of my own trap. A couple of times, I tried to kill him, but failed.

In the end, I decided to live with G.g without knowing why.

Kan is my name.

In fact, few people know who I am. Like a fish out of water, I've dived and struggled to find my way out of the quagmire.

I have a dark life of a fly in a spider's web. It seems to be getting worse and worse. In times of despair, I often wonder if being a part of these pages might help me out of this impasse, or my life might at least be a little bit more bearable.

How hard it is to get out of the quagmire.

Don't rush to trust anyone, don't try to find meaning in actions; maybe they're simply a game, maybe it's all the product of madness.

(A wolf cub)

April 1st

Everyone knew what April 1st meant.

Of course, there were those who didn't know what it was; they probably didn't need to know what it was either.

To a smaller extent, some knew well that April 1st wasn't only April Fool's Day. They always remembered it as the day when Leslie Cheung took his own life.

Of course, not everyone in the world knew who Leslie Cheung was.

April 2nd (2003)

The morning was silent, seen through the small dusty glass window. I opened my phone; there was a message from H: 'this isn't fake news, my dear G.g'. I was dead on my bed like a dry cockroach skeleton. I felt like my body was turning into a bizarre crematorium; the fire kept burning everything from inside out. But my two arms were glued on the bed, cold. A bed sheet with a criss-cross pattern looked like a well-camouflaged predator pouncing on its prey.

From the rooftop, depressing music drooped down, falling with a thin cloud of dust curling in a swathe of milky light. I decided not to open the window.

The morning was silent, seen through the small dusty glass window.

April 3rd-9th (2003)

It was a hellish week.

G.g spent days searching for news about Leslie Cheung's death. The fall of a superstar from the twenty-fourth floor of a hotel in Hong Kong on April 1st, in G.g's mind, was like a marvellous flight into the clouds, forever above the ground. The silhouette blurred, vanished, and then existed only in the mind as negatives. In that faraway universe, the warm body of the poor man floated in giant wind cones, so that he could forever sleep in that silent summer.

Some local newspapers here and there started talking about the incident, jumping to the conclusion that he was obsessed with the characters he played. It was a hypocritical hypothesis.

G.g looked everywhere for the DVD of *Happy Together*, to no avail. He then watched *Farewell My Concubine* five times a day. He slept on the red sofa, flinging his arms around, his face filled with sorrow. It looked like G.g lay dying in a pool of blood.

I couldn't wash away that image. It clung to my brain like oysters to their reef, waiting to scar my soul. From then on I was always scared of red chairs. My nerves couldn't survive another unsolicited flashback.

After a series of disturbed sleeps, G.g looked gloomy and depressed. He quickly decided he should take leave from his job for a while. He was awake all night and stayed indoors all the time. When he was bored with his reading, he took a razor to shave his legs. He shaved so much that I felt it was not before long the thin skin would disappear, leaving behind the naked flesh, from which drops of blood oozed; and then it was anybody's guess: the flesh would also fall down in chunks and curls, until the only thing left was his bare bones. G.g would be no different than a zombie, a skeleton walking on stilts.

Frightened by my own thoughts, I tried to shoo the image away by throwing his razor under the bed.

'You shouldn't shave your legs too aggressively. There's no use. Instead you'd better go to the barber to have your hair cut. You're unkempt, like an orang-utan. Now, stand up.' I said, touching his arms.

'Leave me alone. Did you forget? I'm planning to keep it long so that I can have it permed', G.g argued, his eyes on his legs.

'We need to go out sometimes. It's stagnant here. Why don't we go to the cinema to watch a horror film?'

'No! Those boring films? I'm not interested. By the way, please don't talk about films anymore. I get a fever when it comes to films. I hate watching films now. *Farewell My Concubine* is, and will be, the last film I watch. I don't think I should watch anything else. Enough. That's enough.'

We stared at each other in silence; our tired breaths were audible against the silent midday. I couldn't go out without an unknown fear permeating through the veins under my pale skin.

A moment passed before the phone went off with reminders that I had to go to the ad agency on time, where final touches for in-progress designs were waiting for me.

Holding back a sigh, I shook G.g. 'Are you okay? I left the cakes in the fridge. I'm coming back late. By the way, the paint is already dry on the canvas. I think you'd better keep working on the painting.'

'I know,' G.g cracked a wan smile. 'Go to work, don't worry. Everything's fine, I promise I won't do anything stupid. Sometimes it's good, playing with a razor, isn't it? Look, I have silky legs like a girl.'

I left for the office. On the way my mind was full of G.g. He sat in the foetal position, as lonely as a stray dog. I knew I couldn't do anything to help him. I felt sorry for him. I knew it would take the little dog ages before it knew the way through the vast field when the dark of the night fell.

***

I told myself that I had no reason to be as depressed as G.g was.

I went to work early every day, having bread and coffee for breakfast, trying to stay sane by avoiding the news where headlines broadcast Leslie Cheung's life and death.

Some colleagues passed by, and commented on my hair, newly dyed in pink. They said it went well with my pale skin.

'You really look like a serial killer in a horror film,' Kan laughed.

He had even, pearly teeth, but he looked as fake as a

guy in an ad. I had a theory that he was whitening his teeth once every six months. I really wanted to break all his teeth with a pair of pliers. I would do it slowly, to indulge in the schadenfreude pumping in my body. I would then look at my victim with a sardonic smile while he lay writhing in pain, begging me to let him go. Revenge was sweet.

Trickles of blood would drop down from his neck and cover his muscular chest. Kan had a predilection for clothes in red. I was going crazy at the prospect of what the two shades of red could do when mixed together. I never denied my thirst to kill, especially when I was under attack, although most of the time they were only petty squabbles.

The thought of a heinous crime scene, where I killed, made me pumped. No one should ever think I would feel guilty about it. Never!

1. Chaotic

G.g picked up his brush again and painted more than ever, to the point of madness.

I took refuge in my small room to work on my writing projects, unable to be self-disciplined. I thought one day I'd have to take antidepressants like G.g did. Street drugs, even.

I slept with him three times a week. I was sure it wasn't too much. On the way to his place, I always passed by a convenience store to buy cartons of milk for him to keep in his fridge.

G.g lived in a bungalow on the outskirts of the city. From afar, it looked like a pile of forgotten wooden toys; the ugly garden felt as sticky as the skin of a reptile. Other spaces in the house looked dense, but the bedroom was quite comfortable, as if something surprising might come out unannounced from a corner. So many times I've had to discard used condoms that G.g left under the bed, and I always had to have a tube of lubricant available, for G.g didn't care.

‘Look at my new painting’, G.g said, a smile on his face. Specks of white paint coated wisps of hair on his forehead.

‘You changed the colour?’ I looked at the two shadows as if they were flirting in silence. The summer sky was blurred by a thin cloud of dust; the next second it looked like a gloomy winter day.

‘This type of canvas costs a lot.’ G. g said flatly.

I went around looking at the painting. Three pieces. Sexless phantoms. G.g painted a triptych in a week, a shade of grey with a faint touch of yellow still wet on the canvas. How beautiful.

G.g inserted the straw into the milk bottle, and finished it in a single long slurp. His eyes seemed to be smiling. ‘I threw away the DVD,’ he said. ‘What?’ I was taken aback. ‘That was the best DVD we had.’ I clenched my hand into a fist. G.g’s reason was that he already knew by heart every scene; he didn’t need to re-watch the film any more.

‘It belonged to both of us. But never mind, you should try to forget it’, I said in a thin voice. I hugged G.g and helped him to his bed. He had a slight fever. I stroked wisps of hair on his forehead with the hope that he could sleep better.

From then on, in front of G.g, I tried not to mention Leslie Cheung again.

2. p

'Humans fear solitude. It's solitude that humans do everything to escape from. Many hide from it. Their admission of solitude precipitates pity, or even worse, disparagement, from other members of their communities. They torture others before they find in the mirror their evil faces, trying to persuade themselves that it's only a nightmare.'

He poisoned me with his cheap-ass philosophy. What does 'torture' mean? He was torturing me. I hated him.

3. insecure

I started having more dreams, perhaps because my room was air-conditioned. My sleep was less tiring than last summer.

G.g was busy with shapes and shadows in his paintings,

and we made love less often. I didn't feel sad about that. I was also snowed under with my own projects. In the morning when I woke up by G.g's side, in purity and cleanness, there was something chill wandering in my breath like a harbinger, like when you were swimming in dangerous waters and your instinct told you that you were going to drown.

But G.g drowned before me.

Not in any stream or ocean, but in his bathroom. He had a stomach ulcer, attributed to his alcohol abuse. It was the aftermath of a drinking binge with a group of his friends, perhaps some self-indulgent radical artists, who always wanted to get wasted together; they became their own victims, subservient to their own wacky ideas. G.g had been falling. It was partly my fault. I didn't have enough time to take care of him.

I rushed him to a clinic, paying the extra fee for emergency care. A young doctor performed a very quick check on him, gave him a jab, and then reassured us that, in fact, G.g was fine. He should drink milk in the first two days, and if necessary, he could also have porridge with protein supplements.

I put his meds into my bag, watching him going to the lift in a gleeful, energetic mood. I was worried whether he remembered the doctor's advice. He was forgetful, and I was afraid his condition might grow worse.

I bought two books, one thin, the other thick; one about death, the other about fear, and talked G.g into reading them. He was more interested in the book about fear. He lounged on the red sofa, and reminded me that this month I had to finish four projects to cover the airfares for our sea trip together, which included snorkelling and parasailing too.

Parasailing was G.g's favourite activity; it was his obsession. I believed G.g was suffering from a mental breakdown.

Anyway, I loved two pieces in his most recent triptych. They were wild.

4. wild – my favourite word

People thought I was simple, and a bit unstable. I didn't give a fuck. Caring about what people thought was a waste of time. I had my own goals and principles. I lived for myself and because of myself; I did what was needed to meet what I aspired, demanded, worshipped. I knew I was selfish, but I was happy that way. I only cared about what I wanted, and I took up all its ramifications. Norms belonged to another paradigm that had nothing to do with me. I had my own universe, my own satellites, and I revolved around my own orbit.

'Wild' was my favourite word but it was not always without its problems.

Sometimes, my axis was shifted, or my orbit would get derailed by a sudden collision. It was when I needed H most. I didn't have the ability to resolve the problems of daily life. More often than not, I thought I was more like a poor bug than a human. 'A wretched creature!' H laughed, mocking me. His timely humour tore off the invisible prison cell around me. I admired his spirit. In essence, I knew he was an absolute pessimist struggling with chronic depression. He was masterful in using language. I often attributed a sense of humour and sarcasm with intelligence. I believed he was a master. I loved him more than anyone else.

5. p

'Not every child loves their parents.'

I came to this firm conclusion, because I once saw him disembowel a doll, his eyes bloodshot. His father's name was written on the doll's belly. The doll opened its eyes in terror. He stared at it for a minute and a half. Then he threw the doll into the trash bin. It made a cold sound.

On my porcelain body, he made a long line with a pen.

'I never loved my dad! Sometimes I want to kill him. Am I cruel? I don't know. Do I love my mum?'

He sneered. Was he really interested in the idea? What was it inside that volatile body? He disgusted me, but I learned how to quench my fear in his presence. I knew his secrets. But I didn't do anything.

6. p

MSM

7. p

One night, he came home very late, completely shattered. His eyes were vacant due to sleep deprivation. He hid between his lips a mysterious smile. He got undressed, but as usual he didn't bother taking a shower. He lay face down on the bed, breathing hard. But a few minutes later he jumped on me and made a tattoo on my skin with three letters: MSM.

It was the second time he tattooed these three letters. I didn't get it.

8. p

MSM, MSM, MSM.

He made tattoos in a frenzy. My body was soaked in blood. The blood spread and in the next moment, it covered my body. I was peeled.

9. depressed, uninterested

H brought me some new DVDs with content he downloaded from the Internet. 'For fun', he said, and left. I knew what was in there: chemsex. I didn't need to watch them anymore. I was looking for that real-life satisfaction, one that was always on the brink of turning into disappointment, out there where it was noisy and derelict.

But let's see what he had. LockedUp, a series of bareback porn from Europe.

10. LockedUp

Locked up! How many times did I think about imprisonment? How many times did I imprison my own life? Why couldn't I talk about my soul in no more than a word?

'G.g, where were you last night? Don't tell me you were busy supporting your circle of artists, who can't even produce anything worthy. Come on, where were you?' Your lascivious looks, your posture, I knew everything. Why did you do that to me?

G.g still continued sleeping.

Out there it was as hot as if everything was on fire. The room was already cold—but why didn't dreams come to me?

G.g turned silently in his sleep. At the back of his room

stood a clothes hanger, on which lay the pair of jeans G.g often wore whenever he went to town. Dry trails of sperm were visible in the upper part; they looked like glue.

Out there it was as hot as if everything was on fire.

11. Hot

It was summertime. The heat roasted the city in its crematorium. If I didn't have the air-conditioner, the room would have been an oven.

I went out to a small coffee shop where I read a thin book by a female author with a weird name. There were stories, piles of them; mountains of melancholic text. Her prose was well-polished. There was a line I found interesting: 'Cicadas' calls scratch at a summer's sky'. There weren't many cicadas in the city. Trees covered in dust couldn't inspire art. How did she write that beautiful line? It left a mark in my mind, engraving a line of memory.

12. comrades

She was my best friend, the author with the funny name. I often referred to her as my comrade. But that's for later. For some time before we became close, we had very little contact; we even avoided each other.

I was four years younger than her. We were co-workers. Whenever we met, we even glared at each other. Each word uttered was a barometer of the other's attitude and mood, bit by bit. Why did we live so anxiously and build bunkers to wall ourselves in such a stupid way, to the point of suffocation? I often wondered.

And then we started telling stories that we could laugh at. We became closer that way. At some point I thought the most appropriate word to describe our relationship would be 'comrades'. Comrades were definitely not siblings, not even lovers and not necessarily friends. We maintained our comradeship by doing certain things together. The bond thus developed over time.

We never talked openly about love or gender-related issues. I thought it was to be kept in private, the realm of impregnable secrets. Although she didn't say it, I thought she was smart enough to guess what my sexual orientation was. Yes, sexual preference had nothing to do with morality; we had agreed on that point.

That was how we were comrades.

13. stupid passion

At work, we got to know each other like how a couple of grasshoppers scrutinise each other with their antennae.

In addition to working at the design company, I also had a side job as an illustrator for a women's magazine, where my comrade was an editor of the fashion column. She knew too well various types of lipstick, dresses and hundreds of accessories, but I rarely saw her wearing them. When she had to work outdoors, she didn't even bother to put sunscreen on her small, thin face; with two lines deepening on the side of her nose announcing her anguish. My comrade just needed to put on a dark shabby wide-brimmed hat, like a wilted mushroom, and a cowboy shirt that hung down to the back of her hands, and that would've been it. Her style would have smeared and destroyed the fashion industry. Perhaps she only felt confident when she hid in that mediocrity, in contrast to other women.

I often used riotous colours in my illustrations for articles in cheesy columns. I made a lot of money from the job, enough to buy flamboyant shirts that were just as riotous as the illustrations. I became some sort of queer mutant. In other words, I was a beetle who dared to display its aggressive nature.

Despite our differences in fashion styles, we shared a quirky trait in that we often made some silly life choices, subjecting ourselves to the judgment of those around us. They wouldn't leave us alone; they talked about us all the time. But we flaunted everything; I even set out a life motto to ignore all public opinion. The crushed corpses of public opinion were casually thrown into the dustbin; if they were still alive, I'd pour them on the floor, put gasoline on their backs so they could quickly burn into ashes.

'Too cruel', she grinned happily when she heard me express my thoughts. We just went on with our lives. We defied, as long as we loved.

But what did we do?

I could spend a lot of time for my writing, with the hope that one day I would become a writer like her. But I struggled to write. All I knew was that I loved writing. I had tons of tiny writing worksheets in distorted layouts and crippled grammar structures. I'd like to have them published in a miscellaneous column in a literary journal. But my comrade insisted that it was a fancy definition of 'writing' by delusional writers. I was confused. It struck me that miscellany meant messy, nonsensical writings. I hated this condescending and presumptuous sarcasm, but still I burst out laughing, saying that my writing should really be featured under uncategorised miscellany. Of course, at a fraction of the price of an illustration, it was just enough to give me a little mental comfort.

What about my comrade? She was an affluent writer who couldn't afford to expand her readership. Seemingly unsatisfied with her creative productivity, she plunged into another field in the spirit of a suicide squad member. I didn't understand why she had the idea to write a screenplay, and even dragged me to work with her. A film for sure! I was well aware how disabled this film industry had been for nearly half a century, and even when my comrade was to contribute something to it, its paralysis would not go away either. However, if she liked it, I would support her. Just like how she once encouraged me to produce those pieces of rubbish.

In short, we poisoned the future with self-loathing traps, in the hope of having some fun. No plans, no regrets. Free to be happy.

As believers in foolish pleasure, we deserved support, didn't we?

14. drown the summer sun and then soak it in a pot of poison

Summer was the season I hated the most. I was at home every day. The huge fire pan strained my nerves. Yesterday, the air conditioners were fixed and cleaned, so it was a little bit better. Thanks to cooler air, my sleep wasn't interrupted, but it didn't mean that I could easily visualise my dreams.

There was a clank of a lock downstairs, followed by an

angry clatter of shoes. Maybe H was back. Next, I heard him swearing in a hoarse voice, as if the time he had spent in the hot sun had burned his throat. He opened his eyes to see me lying on the floor, while he gulped down a bottle of water. After a while, it seemed that the cool water had saved his burned vocal cords, and he said, 'Did you get any sleep?' then threw some books on the floor.

H had just returned from an international book fair. I didn't care. Every summer there were countless fairs with exhibitions taking place almost every other week, most of them looking sloppy and chaotic in the literal sense of the words. There were transactions and noises on loudspeakers everywhere, the acrid smell of human sweat, fuming ice cream vending machines smelling of oranges or durian, mixed with the tumultuous sound of shoes on a dusty brick background. All in all, it was typically a messy scene. I got sick every time I thought about it.

'Damn it! I hate summer so much'. H was clearly in a bad mood.

'Just now, walking on the street, passing a fruit stall, I saw a seller using a knife to peel grapefruit. The knife was so big, the steel shining with a cold sharp ray, shining in the sun. It occurred to me: if only I could use that knife to slice the sun into hundreds of pieces. It'd scatter like shards of molten steel in the pit of a forge. Then we can use metal thread to sew those hot shards together and throw them in a bowl of ice water. It will freeze to death there and stop torturing us. The sun deserves it! Hahaha...'

H concluded with a wild laugh. I thought he was going crazy from the heat.

Hahaha... I laughed along; I was as excited as if I had been injected with a stimulant. I loved H's crazy idea. I also had the same hatred for the sun. I thought that one day, I'd gain superhuman powers so I could drown it in a pot of poison.

With the books H brought home, I had something to keep myself busy all afternoon.

Over the next few days, I suffered from anorexia, dozing all day, a book on René Magritte falling beside me. I wished I could free my arms at my sides and fall (or fly?) vertically in the sky like the men in black in Golconda. If the sun were replaced by the cold grey-blue moonlight, I could also fly in a black suit (but definitely not a black felt hat, I hated hats), just like in the painting. I wondered if Magritte dreamed of killing the sun while working on this immortal painting. Rigid effigies multiplied, lying in the contours of the city that were also rigid. Black flies buzzed. Everyone interpreted the painting in the same way. Couldn't people see that those black flies could fly? Personally speaking, just being able to fly, even if I was a dirty fly, was already great. No criticism, no need to wear a black uniform to think. I wanted to stand tall, to throw enslaved thoughts into the sky so that they too could fly away. Magritte—had he ever dreamed of killing the sun like me? I loved him because he made paintings that could fly. I liked Golconda partly because it depicted a green atmosphere. I loved what was pale. Compared to Dalí's furious surrealism, I preferred Magritte, for his hues of sadness, and the dark inhibitions entwined with a lust for freedom in his style.

Around four-thirty in the afternoon, I saw H take out a red plastic basin that I often used for my paint scraps, including rags, used paint tubes, dull brushes, cigarette butts and emptied juice cans. H carefully scraped everything with a thin knife, passed it through a large nylon bag, grabbed its handles, and threw it in the trash. He left the red basin in the hallway, where the sunlight came in, in order to dry the stains inside. He proceeded to tidy up out of habit, so that the next time he drew, everything was as good as new. I was very grateful to him for his kindness.

But now, I found the red basin leaning on one side of the wall shining in the sun really annoying. There was something stirring inside me. I got up, kicked the basin aside; it rolled around. I had a cool idea.

After I filled it with water, I carried the basin out onto the porch. I clearly saw the sun lying in the basin, swaying as if it were laughing. Okay—you, the sun, you will go blind, you will stop making that arrogant face, you will die, one way or another. I will poison you.

Where was the poison? I went back into the house, eager to find a possible solution. But there was only kerosene. What else? It was hard to find something lethal in this house. The refrigerator was stocked with water, milk, and other beverages. If you wanted to kill the sun, maybe you would have to go down the street to buy a bottle of pesticide.

A bottle of poison! As soon as I started to walk, I suddenly felt too afraid to see the light outside still burning bright. If I waited until nightfall, perhaps I would explode. I was still hesitating on the doorstep when H came out of the bathroom, drenched in water. 'Where are you going?' he asked, his eyes widening in surprise when he saw that I was so badly dressed and how my hair was all tousled. I said I was going to buy a bottle of pesticide. When he heard that, he panicked, his face contorted as if he had just been splashed with acid. He ran and grabbed my arm. From the look on his face, I thought it was him who had a mental illness, not me.

I reassured, 'You think I'm going to buy poison to

kill myself? Ah ha. What the hell are you so scared of? Suicide? Never!'

'So what are you going to buy it for? Come on—come back now!' H commanded. Then, holding my hand, he dragged me into the room, and pushed me on the bed. Seeing the bed made me sick—I'd lain on it for many days until I'd thought my body was rotting.

'I hate the sun; I want to drown it in a pot of poison. Look...' I pointed to the hallway, where the hot afternoon sun made the basin red like a furious fire.

H nodded. He wandered around the room for a few minutes to think. His face softened, turning into a sinister sly look. He presented me with a new game, and carefully advised that I could do it at any time when I couldn't control my anger.

The game was as follows: we were to use a jar of Chinese ink mixed with table salt, add a small amount of kerosene to make it smell bad, and then slowly pour the mixed solution into the basin of water with the flaming sun in it. Step by step, the black water drops would gradually spread, invading the whole basin. H and I burst out laughing when we watched the sun being slowly stained, eaten away by the black-smelly-salty solution. Great! We laughed non-stop. No need for pesticides; with just a little creativity in difficult circumstances, we were able to commit a great crime: killing the sun.

In a pool of foul, black water, it would never shine again. It would go blind. Ah ha.

If it lived, it would also flop around, become deformed, choke to death, or become corroded by salt water. Ah ha.

It was about half past five in the afternoon. The last beam of sunlight of the day perished on the side of the door.

I didn't remember what I did after that. Perhaps drowning the sun wasn't all that convincing. I was afraid that it might wake up around midnight, light up again, and then swallow the cold blue moon. It was impossible to live if the night was also burning and roasting. I felt a little uneasy.

I woke up, took all the ice cubes from the fridge and poured them into a basin of black water. I could then sleep soundly until morning. In the morning, if the sun were to rise, I would perform the ritual again. Again and again. Every move was perfect. No details were omitted. Every day, I would create a bunch of different recipes. Strong salt water mixed with a little fish sauce would suffocate it, making its skin sticky; it would then peel off, I thought. The ink drops were really black. While dyeing the sun, if I added a little bit of red—the diluent from the acrylic jar—the red drops would flow like blood. It was spectacular! Another time, I also sprinkled a layer of kerosene on the surface of the water, then turned on the gas lighter and burned it. I quickly discovered that it could cause a fire and damage the plastic basin, and I would have to buy a new one. I couldn't do that again. I then added bleach, wastewater, or, rarely, the tail of a gecko, and dead cockroaches. I threw them all into that pool of black water. It was a disgusting hodgepodge of a recipe, something I came up with in an instant. But the most important ingredients were Chinese ink and pesticide solution. I was satisfied with its black colour. I stored a lot of ink and pesticide in the house for later use. The thought that the sun was stained and suffocated in a pot of poison gave me a peace of mind to work.

I needed to thank H again. He helped me to destroy my enemy and taught me a wonderful, barbaric game. I played it with passion. As long as I lived and the sun was not dead, I would continue.

15. my comrade and films

'Come with me. We'll have the opportunity to collaborate with a famous young director,' she whispered over the phone, trying to persuade me.

We went to a press conference, where they introduced a film project that promised to be the 'masterpiece' of a short, fat director. He bragged endlessly about Kim Ki Duk's art and James Cameron's special effects. I yawned six times in five minutes. I didn't understand what he said about Hollywood's grandiose depiction and Kim's artistic sense. Listening to him talk about his project, I was completely lost. If he were to stuff all of his crazy ambitions into a film in such an awkward way, I believed what he'd make would be a disaster in a film industry that was already disastrous.

Another guy, his colleague, walked with a sideways gait and had a bitter treble voice, nodded in agreement, his eyes had two eyelids that were so puffy that they sagged. He kept looking at that fat dwarf with mockery, a stare that was mixed with contempt and envy. It looked like a dramatic attempt to cover up a very bitter co-worker relationship.

I texted my comrade, 'I feel like throwing up. Look at that puffy-eyed old man's face'. The comrade texted back, 'The young man is better! His saliva is all over the screenplay while he talks. Come to think of it, how are we going to approach that guy?' 'Ha ha...' I twitched the fingers of my right hand to keep my laughter from escaping my mouth. I didn't want to sound rude.

I thought it was much more pleasant to sit and watch a second-rate film than to listen to its creators bragging about it. It was utterly ridiculous.

I suddenly thought of G.g. His stress in the summer might have nothing to do with the sun. Even though the sun was the culprit that gave off the heat that burned the earth, what burned his heart? In a way, his hatred of the sun must have something to do with the problems he had in the past. I never heard him reveal even a small piece of his past. The crazy game of drowning the summer sun in a pot of poison that I had devised, indeed, calmed him down for a while. But what would happen after that? I didn't know; no one could predict anything. Like the flamboyant director, he could not have foreseen his future failures. He was cultivating the rotten yeast of paranoia in his mouth but did not know it. I just realised that G.g seemed to be exaggerating the scale of his problems as well. And I was an accomplice to this dangerously inflated balloon. When would that balloon explode? Would I gain anything from the crumbs of that ball? Emotionally, were G.g and I taking it too far?

It was bullshit. I snuck out of the press conference before it was over. Everyone huddled in there must have been poisoned. I needed to breathe fresh air outside and see the sky to fight against the nausea.

My comrade also snuck out, mocking laughter still lingering on her lips. She was sly, I thought.

The two of us stood on the ledge of the big building, chewing gum and thinking. We were like two sneaky mice that had just left their lair, sniffing with their whiskers, plotting to infiltrate and seize new bait, after being disappointed by what had been on offer. Fortunately, the trap didn't work in time.

'I swear, if I watch the film that these two guys are making, Satan will make me die by vomiting blood.' I said, holding my comrade's hand.

She snapped her fingers, opened her mouth and laughed to the fullest, showing her even but dull teeth. She threw the gum on the tree by the fence, making two young leaves stick together.

The two mice slyly headed out into the street, delighted. I was satisfied since I managed to steal three hours from the design agency this morning.

16. anxiety

I woke up around midnight, after a short nap. I could hear the wind shaking the vines, roaring around the long walls and pounding hard against the window frames.

Perhaps a poisonous wind was lurking in the night, or there might've been an unseasonal thunderstorm, or an unusual tornado.

My phone flashed. It was a message from Kan: 'Make sure to print two copies of each design. I couldn't call you when you left yesterday afternoon. Tomorrow morning our client will want to see them... I still can't sleep. Damn, this client is cranky. May the devil incite her husband to strangle her to death.'

I chuckled. Kan didn't text me often. Our relationship at work rarely went awry; it was mostly indifference. However, working in a team with Kan didn't bring much trouble, as he was responsible and ran everything smoothly. There was only a sense of annoyance, and from time to time annoyance turned into hatred, as he repeatedly remarked that I looked exactly like a serial killer. I hated that kind of ridicule. Did I make people feel different? Did I look like a psychopath? Or a pervert? Damn, that word stabbed me like a sharp knife. I wanted to pull the knife out and stab my opponent. Well, if Kan forced me to be a serial killer, oh well, that sounded exciting, because sometimes I used to work on such projects in my dreams as well. I chased people, raised my weapon, and charged straight at the target. I wouldn't deny that the horror, in some cases, was quite effective as a stress reliever. It was quite interesting to think about a scheme to take revenge on someone. But it might be long before I could become a murderer.

While I was re-evaluating the designs, it occurred to me that this guy, Kan, might as well be a pervert destined for me. If he hadn't had a bad history with bossy clients, he must not have cursed endlessly and compared them to animals. It seemed that in order to find inspiration, he had to curse someone, mock someone, and, well, we had many clients. If my theory was correct, his inspiration must've been endless.

I took the drawings that had already come out from the printer. The colours looked perfect, perhaps because I was less demanding when I was sleepy in the dim blue light from the computer.

Then I turned on the table lamp, and listened to music; and with a cup of coffee, my fatigue was gone. Things were pleasant during the night. Until I discovered an anomaly when I looked closely at the drawing: the red couch arranged in the living room directly struck my eyes, as if it were a threat, stunning me. All my intrusive thoughts returned, with the image of G.g lying motionless on a sofa-shaped red pool of blood.

I had to replace it with another colour: ochre, and then green. It wasn't perfect, but tolerable.

17. a beautiful idea

Like a vampire all eyes for traces of blood, H wandered through room after room. He stopped by the kitchen for a while, deliberating whether he should drink beer or wine, but in the end he chose the half-empty bottle of whisky. He swayed as he walked. Then he flung himself onto the balcony and off to the roof where he stood in the wind. His T-shirt, flying in the night, absorbing the faint light coming from below, looked like insect wings. He was very thin. In a moment of illusion, I thought he came from a painting by Magritte, about to fly (or fall?).

I hid in the dark, silently watching H and waiting with excitement. He stood still; he let the bottle fall along his thighs. It almost fell. It was as if he were glued to the roof. What was he thinking about? When was the thin insect taking flight? Should I help him by going there to push him down? Perhaps with my help, he would have momentum to flap his wings and fly, like a bird or a bat.

I didn't feel guilty when I thought about killing him. I thought it was a beautiful idea, very poetic. Fly. Fly. Fly. I wanted to see how humans fly. I was waiting for a chance, and I would do it.

If his flight failed, I'd succeed him to continue the amazing experiment. The problem was: who would push me down?

Fly. Fly. Fly.

18. night wolf

G.g said that his house was surrounded by wild wolves. I yelled, 'You're crazy!' He affirmed, 'Really,' then breathed heavily into the phone, alarmed. It was about two o'clock at night.

'Do you think you're lost in some wild forest? Listen to me, this is the city, and wolves can only come out of the Discovery Channel.' I reassured him, my eyes still on the computer screen.

'You still don't believe me? They're howling down the street, outside the wooden door. I guess about four or five in all.'

'What do you plan to do? What do you want to do with them?'

'I don't know! I feel threatened. Maybe they're hungry. They might feel cold, too. There was heavy rain in the afternoon, which lasted until the middle of the night. I guess they can't stand the cold.'

'Oh, my God!' I tried to hold back a laugh. I loved G.g.'s imagination, and tried to sound serious, 'So you're calling me for advice on how to defend yourself, or are you seeking aid for those beasts?'

'I don't know. I can't tell the difference between a howl from hunger and cold, a craving for protection, or a craving for fresh meat.'

'Listen, wolves are wild animals. Their ability to withstand extreme weather is almost limitless. The icy mountains covered with snow mean nothing to them. You should remember that we live in the hottest tropical city. And the summer roasting pan has just been put away. Instead of worrying about stray dogs in wolf skins, you should watch more nature documentaries on TV to learn more about these things.'

'But they came here, howling, asking to come in. So are they hungry? Or do they need light?' This silly question proved that G.g. wasn't listening to me. He was busy pursuing his own thoughts.

'It's no coincidence that the people living in the jungle always light fires. Both to keep warm and to ward off wild animals,' I let the game take itself too far.

'They just howled again, this time more tragically. Their breathing's growing weaker. Maybe they're exhausted. Oh, my God, can you please help me to find a way out?'

I shook my head, unable to laugh. Well, I had to go with the flow.

'So let's open the door for them to come in, treat them to a gargantuan feast of canned fish in the fridge, give them a warm blanket, wait for them to fall asleep... and then kill them.' The more I spoke, the more impulsive I became. As soon as I realised that I was tempted by the flow of evil thoughts, and in the end, I had to accept being dominated.

'Kill them? Listen, the wolves are growling, they're scratching their claws against the wooden door. Can you hear them? I think they're desperate. What should I do next?' G.g asked urgently.

I growled, 'Put them all in boiling water!'

'What?'

'Put them all in boiling water! If they're too big and numerous, close the doors tightly and create a perfect trap. Splash boiling water from the edge of the door or pour it down from above. Kill them like sly rats. Never let them escape.'

'Why?'

'You like killing, don't you?'

'But...'

'Don't hesitate! You already killed the sun. Wolves? Think of them as flies or mosquitoes.'

'The sun is something else. It resides in a different domain. But here, they're wolves. Isn't that too cruel?'

'Don't show mercy. Be ruthless first, so as to not be attacked by cruelty. Do it quickly if you don't want them to wake up from a good night's sleep! Otherwise their brutal nature will awaken, and they'll attack you with their fangs, tearing you apart like a chicken salad. Soon your body will be left only with broken bones and bruised flesh. Like a chicken salad, you hear me?'

'Chicken salad... Chicken salad?' G.g stammered.

I couldn't hold back my laughter. This savage game of imagination was gradually torturing and poisoning G.g, paralysing his resistance. On the other end of the line, I thought G.g was going crazy from the excitement. I swore there was no such thing as wolves loitering around G.g.'s bungalow at night. It was just an empty suburb. Wild wolves that appeared in the city? Life was not a Hollywood adventure film. G.g, you've tortured me too much. If I don't finish the design for submission by tomorrow morning, Kan won't leave me alone. His endless swearing would drive me crazy.

'That's right! I'm going to open the door. I remember that when I warmed up my dinner, I seemed to have run out of fish. I probably have to replace it with something. Good God, if you don't get my call tomorrow morning, you should know that the wolves have eaten me all, leaving no trace.'

I slowly let go of the phone, trying to prolong the little time it took to be slow enough to hear the dog barking on the other end of the line. I'd wait until tomorrow morning to check if G.g was still alive. At that moment, I was too tired and had to go to bed.

On the computer, an in-progress design lay waiting.

19. p

He plotted to kill the dogs in the most brutal way I know. Why did he call wild dogs wolves? Only God could know. However, I supposed that he had a reason.

He paced to and fro impatiently throughout the kitchen. It didn't take long for the howling to begin.

He took out two small-sized pressure cookers. He filled them with water, put them on the gas stove, turned on the fire, and then turned the knob to the highest setting. He stared intently at the raging fire. At that time, there was no light in the house. In the dark, his eyes flickered, even redder than fire.

It was quiet outside. Only the sound of the wind blowing in waves penetrated the vines. Anyone who ever came to the wooden house hated that tree. Small spigots on the ground threatened to trip up passers-by. It just seemed dangerous. Someone showed their anger by trampling on those sharp, fringed blades. Others were terrified; they took a detour, avoiding it altogether. I called it the poisonous snake plant. But he loved it. He used to passionately kiss that bunch of vipers every morning. While he kissed them, his nose would bulge; his eyes shut. His hands would caress the viper bush, and they would hug each other, sharing their pleasure. I had never seen such bizarre intercourse between a man and a plant. What kind of deformity would they breed? A plant-animal monster with the body of a snake with a human head, or a human body with four limbs of vipers that grow slender, pointed leaves? Even if my life was thrown away, I would try to see the day when that terrible event unfolded. If you wanted to survive in this house, it was better to think about the absurd all the time.

The hissing of the pressure cooker resounded from the kitchen. I saw him pressing his ear to the wooden door, listening to the sounds outside.

The fire on the stove was extinguished. But his eyes were still wide open. Two red spots emitted long beams of light that scanned the darkness.

He placed a plastic basin in the middle of the room.

I realised that the basin was what he used to kill the sun every day. He dutifully filled the basin with boiling water from the two cookers. Heat distorted the darkness. Again he picked up the kettle. He touched the doorknob with a trembling hand.

Outside, the wind was still howling. It seemed it wasn't only the wind any longer.

'Come on in, dear wild wolves!' His voice hissed through his teeth, louder than the sound of the wind. And suddenly the door opened.

Streams of darkness burst into the house. I jumped off the table and lay shivering on the cold, tiled floor.

20. manic slaughtering

I killed thirteen wolves in one night. It was a great feat. Using boiling water to kill was one of the most creative applications that H taught me. I'd love H forever.

Hopefully I'd get more kills later on.

21. torture the useless

After successfully killing thirteen wolves, I became excited at the idea of killing. My body seemed to float, my eyes dreamy, my heart pounding hard, my lungs full of air. I was more sensitive to colours, especially red.

I decided to change the colour of the living room wall and sketched two more paintings, using red as the main colour. Then I bought a series of clothes in red, among which there was a T-shirt with a picture of a wolf shot in the head while crossing a burned forest, which was in black and silver-grey, with splattered prints. I fell in love with this shirt.

At the same time, I made a breakthrough plan: every week, I should practice killing something spontaneously, no matter what it was, as long as it was done with discipline, focus, and creativity.

The first experiment was a wooden chair. It was too old with a few gnawing marks, scratched paint, and a lot of dirty stains. Therefore, it deserved to die.

I killed it in the following steps:

1. Brought a large butcher knife and cut hard into a chair leg. It took a few seconds before it fell over.
2. Mixed a little red paint, neither too thin nor too thick, and sprinkled it on the broken chair leg, right at the spot where it came into contact with the knife. Effect achieved: the chair was bleeding profusely.

3. Used a rope to tie a chair leg, dragged it to the back corner of the garden, and threw it in the trash. While dragging the chair to destroy it, you should listen to how it moans, sliding on the tile floor. The view from above: a long, bruised blood trail zigzagging from the door, then disappearing behind the canopy at the end of the garden; a mysterious and spectacular scene.

N.B.: while doing everything, I didn't forget to use multiple cameras arranged at different angles to capture all the details. I then transferred them to the computer, edited the images and sound, and saved the video in a separate folder, naming it 'experiment 1'.

Sequentially, there would be 'experiment 2', 'experiment 3'... I planned on killing everything useless in the house one way or another. All useless things deserved to die.

After everything was done, I enjoyed a cold beer and went to bed, waiting for H to come back. In the late afternoon, H would appear and hug me like always. The two of us would lie on the floor, with books, tapes, and food all around. While he stroked my hair, I would brag about my achievements. I seriously believed he would be shocked. Hopefully he wouldn't fall over, like a chair.

If he fell, would he become disabled? I'd drag him to

the end of the garden, wouldn't I? I wasn't sure I'd find a way any time soon.

22. imprisoning a puddle

There was a small ditch with a meagre flow near my garden, the result of indifferent urban planning. With tree leaves falling to create a thick layer of humus, I hoped that in the near future, the ditch would be levelled. By that time, I wouldn't have to buy mosquito repellent anymore. The mosquitoes used to disturb my siesta, but thankfully, I got a malaria jab.

A small pond had formed in the garden from the unseasonal rain. Muddy puddles were ideal places for mosquitoes and frogs to breed. I planned to fill them with soil. But H stopped me. He said, 'We can put some lotuses in there, or water lilies or some water hyacinths. Their purple flowers will bloom and decorate the garden.' I endorsed his beautiful idea.

H took me to pick water hyacinths in a river far from the city. There, lotuses and water lilies grew indiscriminately. The smell of mud rose up. I liked being close to wild things.

Despite our best efforts, the pond project failed. The water lilies died immediately, and the water hyacinths perished quickly afterwards. All of them denied survival, like a mass suicide. I didn't understand why: perhaps the water was too polluted, or I didn't grow them properly. What about the water hyacinths? I had carefully picked them up, with their black roots still intact. I had seen them living well despite being crowded together in a tiny ceramic pot in coffee shops. It was crazy.

The pond suddenly stood bare in the garden, in its original form as a disgusting puddle of mud. Frogs left for another place, and the mosquitoes' larvae turned into adult mosquitoes and flew straight to the tree canopy.

I went into the storeroom looking for a shovel. It had been sitting there, rotten, for a long time. When I pulled it out of the door, just exposed to the light, the blade almost fell off, melting into a pile of rust, as red as a nest of fire ants. I threw the dust into the pond. There was a thin layer of scum on the water. With stagnant water below, it felt like the body of water was completely sealed off. To escape from its damned life, it had to evaporate through tiny fistulas that couldn't even be seen with the naked eye.

Standing in the hot midday sun, I looked at the muddy water for a long time, wondering whether I should pour it down the small ditch in the garden. I felt pity. Should I let it flow into another life in prison?

I decided to imprison the puddle.

23. an orphan gift

While working, Kan kept talking about his family, specifically his recently strained relationship with his mother, because of a dog. I'd never heard such a funny story. Just thinking about the scene of a single young man in his thirties, fiercely arguing with an old lady with a grumpy face and sharp words, I couldn't help but laugh. However, as always, to avoid being cursed into an animal, I just listened.

Female colleagues hid their smiles behind computer screens, eagerly waiting for the story to come to a dramatic conclusion. When Kan suddenly stopped, one cheekily encouraged, 'And then what?'

Kan paused for a few seconds, took a sip of water, and continued lamenting, 'It's no good, you know. The house is already cramped, and there's no yard, but that dog went and gave birth. And I don't understand why a black-spotted white-haired mother dog as beautiful as a dairy cow...'

'Ah!' The female co-workers shouted in unison, interrupting Kan, perhaps too amused by the bizarre comparison. Another girl couldn't help but say out loud, 'Yes, such a beautiful dog, your mother must have loved it, or else it would have been killed a long time ago.'

'Oh, that's right!' Kan continued, looking elated. 'That beautiful barking cow could somehow be with some dark male dog, a choice out of blind love. Then what happened? A puppy, one hundred percent black. Well, seeing that filthy black mass wailing and yelping in the cardboard box like a blind rat, I thought it was disgusting. It's unfair to say that it has no eyes, but indeed, a new-born puppy can't open its eyes. In short, I can't stand it. So I secretly threw it on the sidewalk. But my mother found out and she brought it back in. Her face had crumpled as if it had been dipped in acid; she loudly criticised my callous behaviour. She threatened me, saying that if I continued to think of abandoning that poor creature, I would be properly punished in the next life, most likely damned to be an orphan. Damn it! A mother would callously curse her son like that just out of pity for an ugly dog. How is that acceptable?'

No one dared to laugh any more. But I immediately found the key to his temperament, to better understand why he liked to curse with malicious words. Such things passed from mother to child.

'And then what? How did you treat the dogs? And what happened next with your mother? You gave in to her, right?' said a girl, unable to quell her curiosity.

'Well, it's not that I don't love dogs, but I don't accept

ugly things in the house. I'm still thinking of how to get rid of it. Now I'm mad—I'm a high-voltage wire. So please don't touch me or you'll be shocked to death!'

'Oh!' The girls cried out, not daring to say anything more. I guessed they were taking their time for the most sarcastic comments, which they would be ready to say at lunchtime, in Kan's absence.

I glanced at him; he was undeniably handsome. How perfect and lovable he would be if he kept his mouth shut. However he was always an over-sensitive, overreacting urchin. He was like a hedgehog that walked slowly, one that would curl up as soon as it saw danger. Then no one would dare to step on it, or if they did so by accident, they would no doubt be hurt from its quills. In general, he might be unpleasant, but he was ultimately safe to be with. That was how Kan was.

But let him be. I wanted to be different from my colleagues. I didn't like being hurt at work. The successful ones at work were those who knew how to avoid being hurt. Anyway, I was still influenced by him in some way, as I couldn't stop thinking about what he said: 'I can't stand ugly things in the house.' It must be exhausting to be a perfectionist, even just in thoughts. Perhaps he was asking for too much, so he was still single. He deserved it!

While he was trying to think of a plan to deal with the

unfortunate dogs, I came up with another good idea.

At the end of the work day, I poked Kan's shoulder, saying, 'Hey, give me that black puppy!'

Kan stammered, his eyes widened in shock, 'What? What did you just say? You want that filthy black dog?'

'Yes', I insisted, whispering in Kan's ear, 'Give it to me. Everything will be resolved. You won't have a reputation as a pet killer, and I'd have something cool to give my best friend.'

Kan heaved a sigh of relief, his eyes sparkled. 'He likes to keep dogs? That's good. Come over to my place, then. Maybe you'll be able to convince my mother, so that she won't suspect that we are colluding in a conspiracy. You and my mother are indeed similar in your kindness. I hope your friend takes care of that big rat and doesn't turn it into a nasty wolf.'

In the afternoon, I brought the carton box with 'the wolf' inside to the suburbs. I gave that gift to G.g. G.g fell in love with it right away.

We thought for a while, and then agreed to name the little dog 'Wolf', in the hope that it would be strong and brave. I wanted to give it a good life.

24. poisonous mushrooms

G.g took good care of the wolf. He fed it with milk several times a day. The cub was hungry: it drank and then fell asleep. While feeding the cub, G.g didn't forget to stroke it, his eyes narrowed gently, emitting small warm sparks. Sometimes, he would even coo... as if he were soothing it. Other times, it sounded like a lullaby filled with tenderness. I noticed that the wolf's fur was thicker and darker, covering most of the white belly with tiny red blood veins. I thought the wolf would open its eyes in about three days.

However, the wolf didn't know of the danger lurking behind the kind hands that fed it every day. Its fate was decided on the very day it opened its eyes to see the light. The world wobbled around as G.g smiled to the little eyes that had just opened slightly, declaring, 'Dear wolf cub, I will kill you when you turn a year old!'

The dog barked, oblivious to the brutal threat. It wagged its tail and ran to the porch, happily smelling the cool, moist air after the rain. The peaceful world was opening its doors to it and would close on this day, one year later.

I was shocked and sat down on the red sofa that I hated. I stared at G.g, who was using a red marker to cross out today's date on the calendar on the wall. I knew I couldn't stop his madness. However, I planned that when the day came to execute the little creature, I would save it again, just like how I saved it from Kan's evil hands.

Why did I always make friends with violent people like Kan and G.g?

While the wolf ran around exploring, G.g and I went to the garden. We carried large butcher knives. We planned to check and clear the garden. I discovered that there was a broken chair lying on the trash bin, full of green moss, decaying. I brought fallen branches to cover it, a useless thing that deserved to be buried and forgotten.

We took a look around. The wolf followed. I sat down and stroked its forehead. My heart was filled with love for it. It stood still, tongue sticking out, eyes blinking gratefully, tail wagging happily.

G.g was trimming a tree branch. The knife was thrust deep in the wood; the sap was oozing out of the branch, crystal clear. After being exposed to the air for a few seconds, it turned green. G.g pulled out his knife and collected a stream of green sap on its tip. He dripped a few drops on the wolf's head. The wolf was startled and backed away, barking noisily. It ran as fast as it could into the house, shaking its head while running. Poor thing—the sap had clung to its sparse hair, and couldn't be shaken off no matter how hard it tried. It kept rubbing its head on the ground and rubbing against the wall, using both front paws to scratch at its sap-stained fur, but it became even worse.

A chill ran down my spine, as if the point of the knife was also dripping sap onto my bare back.

G.g pointed the wet tip of his knife at a rotten log, narrowed his eyes, and shouted, 'Look, there're so many wood ear mushrooms. It's only rained a few times and they have grown so much. Soon this garden will be covered with mushrooms. Let me think—can we make a dinner with mushrooms?'

'Yes, if you'd like to', I agreed reluctantly. After a moment's hesitation, I said, 'Actually, I don't like black wood ears. Eating them is like eating cat ears.'

'Oh my good Lord!' G.g laughed, 'That's why it's called black wood ear mushrooms. But don't worry. We'll cut those ears thinly when preparing them. Do you know how to prepare bitter melon soup? People cut open the bitter melon, stuff it with a mixture of minced meat, vermicelli and finely chopped black wood ears.'

I was dumbfounded. I watched as G.g pulled out the mushrooms and piled them up on the ground. I thought that I should go to the kitchen to get the basket. Anyway,

I swore never to eat those hideous mushrooms.

When I came back out, I saw G.g with his back to me, ducking into the bushes, looking for something. I warned, 'Watch out for spiders! Snakes and insects, too.' G.g was silent, throwing a few small white mushrooms dotted with light black spots behind him. With no knowledge, I couldn't determine what kind of mushroom this was. Out of boredom, I shouted, 'It's a poisonous mushroom!'

'You're crazy!' G.g crawled out of the bushes, smiling cheerfully, 'I'll admit I'm stupid about animals, but I'm sure I have some understanding about plants. These are termite mushrooms, straw mushrooms and snow fungus, and they're all edible. Poisonous mushrooms are often colourful.'

'Really?' I doubted him. With my little knowledge of botany from high school, it was probably not one of the three mushrooms that G.g just named. I held it up to examine it, wondering, 'But how do you rule out the possibility of a poisonous mushroom disguised by its pretty appearance? On the Discovery Channel, you can see that ocean creatures also change according to the environment to survive. Even a tree knows how to trap its prey and then secrete poison to soften its body, and then eat it at its leisure.'

G.g dropped the knife and smashed it, jumping up

and down shouting, 'Ah! That's a great idea. What did you just say? Camouflage? Okay, we're going to "cover" these mushrooms. Thank you very much.' G.g hugged me tightly, kissing me hard. He bit my ears like how he'd eat a black wood ear.

So, all afternoon, I was dragged into this crazy game of his: we went to find mushrooms and disguised them.

The visual trick was as follows:

1. We used bright colours such as red, pink, orange, and yellow, to paint on the white mushrooms we just found. On one condition: the mushrooms should be capless. If the cap came loose or had wilted, it had to be destroyed immediately.

2. For black mushrooms, or those dotted with black or mixed with a lot of grey, we sprinkled fresh colours such as green, blue or moss green on them. Seeing them change colour, we screamed and laughed in excitement. 'Oh look—moss has grown on the mushroom caps!'

3. For poisonous mushrooms that we identified, we carefully dyed them in white paint; sometimes it took two or three times to completely cover them in white. Just like the first group, the old mushrooms were killed.

We worked meticulously.

Of course, we took turns recording all of these games on camera.

Sometimes, even we got confused. Like some kind of mushroom that didn't really have buds, nor did its cap really open, but its whole body was covered with a white thread like silk. Under the cloak that covered their heads, they looked sullen and melancholic, but when the light hit them, their beauty shone. I gave them a suitable name: the bride mushroom.

G.g was to take it out from the ground, but I stopped him. He crouched down, staring at it, grimacing, 'So we have to find a groom for the bride, right? Let's see.'

G.g looked around and found a black mushroom that was hiding in the shade. It looked scared. He carefully plucked the root with the moist soil underneath, and transplanted it next to the bride mushroom. Clasping his hands together, G.g nodded happily, 'Come on, cuddle. I let you guys breed freely!'

We laughed, picked up butcher knives, and swung them in the air, slashing wildly. We danced, enjoying the deformed mushroom garden. Crazy colours lurked in the leaves, on the rotten logs, on the ledges, in the dirt, in the garbage pits. They all shook their heads because they were oppressed and humiliated. It was fine as long as we were happy. We made torture fun. The next morning, we would wake up early to see the mushroom garden unfurling. The camouflage would be much more beautiful than this. How wonderful!

I had a dream that night, a dream of having a lunch full of 'poisonous mushrooms'. My colleagues screamed in terror while I happily popped the colourful mushrooms into my mouth, munching on them. I wouldn't die—I knew that for sure. People around me wouldn't understand, and they'd think I had magical powers. People would whisper to each other, 'Look, that psychopath consumes poisonous mushrooms without dying. Don't believe me? Look!'

Oh, long live poisonous mushrooms!

I was tempted by the dream of eating poisonous mushrooms. I closed my eyes and enjoyed it. Should I share this dream with G.g?

25. story of a dark horse on the mountain

When we were at work, Kan suddenly asked, 'Is the dog that you brought home for your friend still alive and well, H?'

The rattling of the computers in the room stopped.

All the female colleagues turned to look at us. I could see through their thoughts unfurling behind those blank, blinking pupils. They knew too well that anything from Kan could become material for gossip during lunch breaks.

One of the girls in the room asked, 'Wasn't that your dog, Kan? The one that you threw on the sidewalk without your mother's knowledge? Is it still alive?'

Kan lowered his head, pretending to be working, but he couldn't hide his irritation. His hands hesitated on the keyboard, dragging the mouse slowly as if he were searching for words to retaliate. Moments of silence passed, and Kan still didn't react in his usual snappy manner. He let out a vague sigh filled with disappointment.

Another girl asked, 'I think keeping an animal is a big deal. But we aren't always ready. Kan, have you abandoned it already? Or have you given it to H? Isn't that right, H?'

The ball was in my court, and the conversation unfolded awkwardly. I briefly told them how I asked G.g to take care of it. I shared my frustration with Kan, but I still secretly blamed him. The little dog thing was sort of a deal, a private matter between me and Kan. Why did he have to bring it up here and now? Didn't getting the dog out of the house give him some relief? It turned out that he still remembered that dog. Or was he feeling some remorse?

'Why don't you get married, Kan?' another voice giggled, changing the subject but continuing to tease him.

She was a famous seducer: twenty-four, beautiful and flirty, known for her collection of lovers. There wasn't much diversity in those men, however, because they were always big, dark-skinned guys.

Kan moved his body, tapped the armrests of his chair with his fingertips, calmly said, 'I think I've had to endure one terrible woman in my life—my mother—and that's enough. I have a very bad impression of women. I don't like them at all.'

'Hey, hey', the seductress raised her voice, leapt out of her chair, and moved quickly across the room like an unbridled horse. Everyone had their eyes on her. 'If you don't like women, people would think you're gay.'

'Fine then!' Kan leaned on the chair, straightened his arms and legs, stretched his facial muscles as if to show that he was relaxed. His eyes narrowed defiantly, a way of showing contempt; he continued, 'I'd rather hang out with muscular guys than with girls. At least they can play games with me; they can help carry things up and down a few floors without getting tired. They can also trim trees, fix electrical appliances, and wash cars, and—especially—they don't whine, make a fuss, or gossip. Like you!' Kan said loudly, emphasising the last two words.

The whole room was silent. Indeed, it was truly brave of him. His fierce response to our female colleague's provocation was cathartic. The defeated seductress, her face pale, immediately retreated to her seat, not forgetting to blurt out a weak, sarcastic remark: 'Kan, you're a one-of-a-kind pervert.'

Kan clasped his hands together and laughed. Everyone laughed. The ebullient atmosphere seemed to ruthlessly undercut the seductress' belligerence.

Everyone was energised and kept on working. I changed my new design with the orange hue, and felt satisfied. But I still felt a little bit uneasy about why Kan suddenly asked about the little dog. Did he feel guilty about it?

At lunchtime, when we were sitting alone at the same table, I approached him directly. Kan, without hesitation, replied immediately, 'Why should I be sorry for what I threw away? I just wanted to ask about its fate. I think it's lucky that you have your friend to take care of it. I'd rather worry about my own fate. If it doesn't die, perhaps in the next life I won't become an orphan, according to my mother's curse. Honestly, I can't imagine what that ugly rat of a dog would look like now that it's grown up a bit. Well, it doesn't matter how big it is, I'm sure it's ugly with that black fur. Let's not worry about this anymore, okay?'

I was terribly disappointed with his explanation.

However, when I looked deep into Kan's eyes, I assumed that he hadn't brought it up just to ask. Something must've happened between Kan and the little dog. No matter how bad the memory had been, it left a mark on you, didn't it, Kan?

In the middle of the meal, Kan rested his chin on his chopsticks, looking into the distance beyond the glass window. The autumn sky bloomed with white, quiet clouds. Banana trees lined the terrace of the shop opposite, showing off their large, shiny green leaves, reflecting the waterfall of sunlight flowing from above like golden honey. A large banana with purple-pink flower buds. At the bottom of the root, there was also a sharp young shoot, turning from white to blue, still tender. Kan stared at the healthy bud, his throat protruding, moving up and down. I noticed that Kan's eyes were discoloured.

'Why are your eyes so red? Do you have an eye disease?'

'No. It's just because I haven't slept for several nights in a row.'

I couldn't contain my curiosity, 'What do you do when you can't sleep, Kan? Do you read a book? Watch a film? How about sitting down to make a design, or going online to relieve stress by sexting? Or do you just lie down and curse the slow passage of time?'

'You', Kan laughed. He quickly wiped the food off his mouth with a tissue and took a sip of water. He adjusted his sitting position, looking relaxed, and asked, 'So what do you think I do?'

'Hold on', I watched his facial hair run wild across his jaw, a strong, square chin. 'Let me guess—I hope you don't get mad. Sex chat?'

Kan chuckled, raised his arms in surrender, and then smoothed his short hair. I discovered that Kan's right earlobe had a tiny hole.

'You think I'm that silly? I'm not addicted to sex. If I want to, I just need to visit a discreet massage spa, an hour or two, and that's it. I do it all the time after work, on the way home. To be honest, for me, it's just an instinctive act to release energy—what I need is something else. I think everyone has been like that. Surely you're not an exception, right?'

I remained silent. Much of my experience so far had mostly been with G.g. Some quick sex somewhere in a karaoke room, a hotel room, an inn, an isolated hut, a suburban garden café, the dressing room of a swimming pool, or in a dark film theatre—and not to mention my bedroom—but I kept it to a minimum. All of that was insignificant to me. Sometimes it was done quickly in fifteen minutes; sometimes it lasted for a few hours. The pose changed at any time depending on the location. At some places we stood with our hands against the wall, at some places we stooped with four legs like animals on carpeted floors, at some places we had to half-stand, half-sit, tilting our legs on the seat, sometimes lying on a chair, at some places we curled up on a cold, inflated mattress. Although I'd experienced many different situations and had many options, they all came to a common end: a feeling of boredom and numbness just a few days later. In the end, I decided to stop having fun with strangers altogether. Because the deeper I went into that rabbit hole, the emptier I felt. Just numb: a bad state born out of bad choices. The faces that I met only for a moment didn't even leave a trace in my memory; they were scattered, blurred with the dance of hands over the skin in darkness.

I believed that no matter how great the function of tongues was, they still couldn't replace the hands. The flexible movement of a tongue transmitted the strongest, most essential pleasures, and played the most important role in erotic stimulation, but they were often confused with each other. Eventually, they were blended together in one's breath, mixed with perfume, tobacco, alcohol and candy. Hands alone could help us discern how each person cuddled, much more than a tongue could. Holding, groping, rubbing, and stroking were some of the most significant things in life. The electrical impulses from those unfamiliar hands passed into my memory, trying to anchor onto something there. Yet they still left me in the end, they clung loosely and then quickly fell out of the folds of the brain. When I was bored and had nothing to do, I tried to pick them up from the stream of old memories, but I ultimately failed, because they were all blurred together. I couldn't distinguish the silhouette of one guy from the other guy. I couldn't even remember the shape of their hands, short or long, with five or six fingers, chubby or sinewy, rough or gentle. There was nothing that I could remember. Just nothing. They soon vanished into thin air like evaporated water. To me, aside from G.g, the other guys I met were all invisible.

Should I reveal all these secrets to Kan?

'No one would've guessed that I'm a film addict. Sometimes I read books. The books I choose are often exceptional. Well—let me tell you. There is one book I find very impressive.'

'Tell me!' I said.

'It goes like this: a man, no longer in the prime of his youth, for reasons not made clear, chose to live as a recluse in the mountains with an old black horse. He took good care of the horse, and the horse also fulfilled his transportation and cargo needs. Life went on smoothly. They understood each other like soul mates. Together they walked through the crossroads of life. That same year, the cold winter came early on the high mountains, precipitated by hail and then an unusually thick fog. The dry grass was running out. Food reserves for both man and horse were exhausted. One night, tears suddenly welled up in the horse's eyes; it looked at its master with an incomprehensible look. He realises that the animal was too old—it was dying. If it didn't die of old age, it would die of hunger and cold. Suddenly the horse came forward, rubbing its muzzle against its master's crotch. Then, do you know what happened?'

Kan stared at me, his already red eyes turned even redder. I saw a pool of blood in those eyes. I shook my head, picturing a strangely sad story.

'The man made love with the dark horse. Only then does the book reveal that it was a stallion.'

'Good Lord!' I froze, my whole body shivering. My throat was bitterly thirsty.

'You know how they made love?'

I stared at Kan's face, but I couldn't really see anything. It was like there was a layer of fog in front of my eyes, quiet and illusory. I reached out and touched the glass of water. It wobbled; I tried to keep it from falling over. I was well aware that my fingers were betraying me; they were twitching uncontrollably.

'The horse stuck its tongue out and wrapped it tightly around the man's thigh, licking his dick repeatedly. The man knelt down, grabbed the horse's huge, long penis and stroked it. They did this for hours, many times that night, and the man, clutching the horse's ragged mane, slept soundly on the only haystack that remained. Outside, it started to snow.'

My heart almost stopped beating. I wasn't really sure what I was thinking. But how could I think?

'That isn't the end of the story. The next morning, the horse was gone. When the man woke up, curled up tightly in a thick cotton shirt, rubbing his eyes, he realised that the horse had taken off the reins on its own and disappeared from the stable some time ago. He looked for it everywhere in the bone-chilling cold. A week later, he discovered the horse's body frozen next to a rocky ridge. Its mouth was tightly clamped on the woollen scarf he used to wrap around his neck to keep warm, the same scarf he used to wipe off both of their semen when they had sex. The old man hugged the dead horse, his face expressionless. Perhaps he couldn't cry, or perhaps the cold had frozen the muscles in his face and the rare tears of old age, causing them to halt abruptly on the inner membrane of his eyelids. He then returned home, gathered the hay and all the logs he could find. He piled them around the horse's carcass, and lit a fire. Then he slipped inside the burning logs, lying next to the horse. They stayed there together, warm. It was still snowing around them.'

The story had come to an end. The lunch break was over. I couldn't finish my food. While Kan was calm, something inexplicable occurred in me. It was like a powerful shock. Something strange, like a wall, seemed to be stuck in my throat, blocking everything I wanted to put in my mouth. It took my breath away.

Kan drank the rest of the water, smiling incredulously while his eyes were still on the banana trees on the porch, where the green sprout had just emerged proudly, straight, smooth, and shiny. In a hallucinatory flash, I saw a black horse appear by the banana trees. The animal stuck out its tongue to bite the vertical shoot, and in front of me, Kan suddenly transformed into the form of an old man on the mountain, melancholic and miserable.

How could I record Kan's transformation into someone else? And the transformation in myself too?

After paying, we walked out in silence. There was only the sound of shoes creaking steadily on the floor. I knew the deep depression lurking in each of those resounding noises.

On the way back, my stomach was in turmoil. I couldn't stop myself from wondering what was hidden behind Kan's story. Was it simply a metaphor for love, lust and solitude? Was it possible that in that lonely setting in the cold high mountains, a man was the same as a horse and a horse was the same as a human being? Maybe I was mistaken.

But why did Kan tell me this story?

26. regrets

People often complain that a year goes by too quickly. But for me, it often feels too long.

Throughout the past year, there were no significant incidents or events. After work, I didn't say goodbye to my colleagues; I just got on my motorcycle and left. After leaving any group of people, I immediately reverted to my original position, the position of an individual-object. That rapid qualitative change was the result of a metaphysical needle being inserted into my body, draining the blood, and then pumping air in. I'd become an empty shell, a lifeless corpse, a hollow carcass. I'd be nothing but an empty nylon bag dragged along by the wind.

Twice a week, that nylon bag would go to the supermarket and wander among the shelves, a ghost in the eyes of others. The ghost gathered everything he needed, put it in a cart, and walked out to the counter.

I'd go home, turn on the TV, take a shower. I'd prepare my own dinner and chew lazily in silence. I often wouldn't finish my meal. I'd share food with the old dog. I listened to the dog barking but didn't care about why it barked. I sat around idly. Sometimes I worked. I brushed my teeth. Then I'd turn off the TV. I'd go to bed. I didn't think about anything. Empty. Numb.

Completely numb.

The next morning the alarm would go off. I'd get up and get ready. I'd prepare breakfast for myself and the dog. I'd get changed and go to work. I opened my mouth. I talked and laughed. I was grumpy and eloquent. I played the role of someone else.

In the afternoon, the cycle would repeat. It was a vicious circle. The spiral went on and on, to the depths of loneliness. Numb.

Absolutely numb.

Then the dog died, in silence, due to old age. I buried some of its personal belongings, its sleeping mat, a jingling rattle, a silver chain, bathing soap, and a drinking pot. But I kept its bowl.

Days after the dog's death, when having dinner alone, I didn't forget to scoop a portion into its bowl. I wandered around in my memory. I remembered how the dog used to bark, and the barks were hard and exhausting. I also remembered now how I was curious about what those barks might have meant. Unfortunately, I couldn't understand them.

Did anything about the dog leave a mark on my memory?

I still asked myself the same question every time I sat down for a meal but I couldn't find an answer. Memories were so far away. They were just barren bits that couldn't be brought back to life; or perhaps I didn't know how to excavate them. My apathy destroyed everything. In the warmly lit kitchen, I could still feel the darkness creeping in; sticking out its tongue, licking around, and soon enough, it swallowed the lamp and took over the room.

I sat in silence in the surrounding darkness, painfully aware that night was darker without the dog's barking. Compared to humans, a dog's life is too short. When would it be my turn? I wondered.

That used to be how my life was: G.g! That was a long year when I didn't have H. But was it really me, G.g?

27. p

He sat in the house, flipping through old postcards. I didn't know what they possessed; what kind of sad memory or remorseful feelings could make him sniffle from time to time? I didn't think he was crying. I always suspected that those of a sadistic nature could never cry nor repent.

From the wooden table, the sky looking through the small window was just a tiny piece of blue, like a child's clumsy collage. I thought someone had drawn the clouds with a white chalk, highlighted the pale blue background, and then attached the craft paper to the wall. In many cases, the world seen through a small window always brought out misperceptions.

I knew because he used to draw many things on me.

He stopped torturing the postcards. He lay on the bed. The sniffling sound was still there. He mumbled something in between his sobs, probably 'Kan'.

I didn't think he was crying.

28. Kan's eyes on a dark rainy afternoon

The company cut off the power around four o'clock in the afternoon. It was pouring rain: the aftermath of a tropical storm. The grey sky, through the glass window, appeared magenta. The dark world without computers prevailed. The female colleagues hurriedly packed up their bags and left.

Kan was still there. He sat motionless in his chair, one hand resting solemnly on the table, like a statue swallowed by darkness.

I didn't want to go home either. There were traffic jams, flooded roads, thunder and lightning, big trees knocked down by the wind; even power lines could suddenly break and fall. The prospect of calamities prevented me from stepping out into the street. Besides, I wasn't going to be busy when I got home. There was no one waiting for me at home. Single life was less troublesome, but occasionally watching your shadow move on the empty wall of a cold apartment also created a sense of frustration. There were canned food, pieces of pre-seasoned meat in the fridge, slices of bread, juice, soy milk, fresh milk, beer, cucumbers, tomatoes, and peppers, cans of beans and mushrooms with a shelf life of six months, tropical vegetables and fruits. All would be used for a lone diner. There would be a mix of laughter and crying from the TV, the noise from the automatic vacuum cleaner, and the air conditioner. The oven hadn't been cleaned for a long time. There was a washing machine with soap stains. There were messy wardrobes, mouldy blankets, and sad pillows. The hot tub would be scalding hot, the shower lazily spewing, the water heater surreptitiously spewing vapour in time with the rhythmic music that came from a small speaker on the ceiling. The stunted vines hung resignedly by the window. My plans were piled up in my brain, amounting to nothing. Was that my life? It was a boring world. If I didn't need to rest, I wouldn't have to return to that place. With my busy work life, I wouldn't have to name that sorrow of solitude. But actually I was just denying the reality. I remembered that that night, according to my schedule, I didn't have to sleep with G.g.

Darkness had now gleefully invaded the room. I still struggled in my own thoughts and refused to return to the place that took me years to build.

Hearing some movement, I turned to look; Kan was still sitting on the chair. Unlike me, Kan had a family, so why hadn't he left?

I nudged Kan's shoulder, softly saying, 'It's late. Aren't you going back?'

Kan raised his eyes in the dark and said with his deep voice, 'Shall we go get something to drink? I'm free.'

I nodded. This was my first time going out with him.

That night, I drove Kan back to my house. I didn't know what time it was, but it must have been very late.

We were drunk. He wanted to sleep at my place. The rain gradually let up.

The room was very warm that day. The blanket covered us. Years later, whenever I remembered that fateful night, my memory was always of Kan's sad, tearful eyes looking at the rain.

29. early morning singing

'Thoughts leave me, like bread crumbs from breakfast. I tidy up the dining table, and then I wash the tablecloths and carpets. Cups, pots and pans, grease stains on lapels. I get rid of all doubts and worries. I push away my connections. The peaceful evenings leave us in droves. Early in the morning you will carefully pack your thoughts and put them in the freezer. The refrigerator is tight. A dull soul is scattered on the roads leading to the suburbs.'

I always remembered the image of G.g singing on the wet roof, his legs crossed halfway as if he wanted to sit on the balcony, where the viper tree spread its tongue to lick his body. G.g's voice was full of wind in the early morning, clear and succulent. Did he climb onto the roof and sit motionless all night?

From the night I drove Kan home, I began to learn how to hide my true thoughts from G.g. I thought I didn't need to mention my betrayal; I didn't want to hurt myself.

The phone rang. I turned and said to G.g, 'I'm going to work. Are you okay? Remember to eat all the yoghurt you put in the upper shelf of the refrigerator. It'll expire next week. Also, it's been raining a lot these days, you should dress warmly. Well then, here I go. Oh, you want to hear a new R&B record? At lunch break today, I'm going to the mall to buy something.'

G.g didn't look back; he said nonchalantly, 'Don't worry, go now or you'll be late. I can watch the news on TV for fun.'

When I closed the door, I still heard G.g's voice in the air, '...In the morning, you will carefully pack your thoughts and put them in the freezer. The refrigerator is tight. The dull soul is scattered on the roads leading to the suburbs...'

On the road, I wasn't sure if I was sad. I was learning how to pack up my false thoughts, put them in the freezer, and let the dull soul leave G.g. The wind was gone; why was the cold still playing on my skin?

30. solitude

When H left, I had only one thought: I must kill the

sun. Darkness was the only thing that brought H back to me; only in the dark could I possess H. Like vampires, we only existed in the dark. When the sun shone, two of us became one, only me. Every morning, I painfully watched him hurry away without knowing what to do. I was powerless, because I was robbed of all my emotions and love. I became lonely.

On one occasion, out of fear, I had only one wish to take H with me, forever. Was there any other way other than killing him?

I was in my own thoughts while the vipers were gently sticking out their tongues to caress my bare feet. I heard the wolf cub purr below. I went back downstairs and prepared breakfast for both of us, canned meat for the cub and 'poisonous mushrooms' for me.

While eating, I whispered to him, 'Eat a lot, dear wolf. In a year, I'll throw you in a pan of boiling oil. At that time, how much will you weigh? Fifteen, twenty kilos, or more? But surely you will turn into a four-legged donut. I'm going to eat my first wolf-shaped donut. I'll be so happy!'

The wolf cub finished eating, licking around the edge. Satan, how shiny his fur was. I cuddled it. It barked as if in gratitude. Animals were less treacherous than humans.

I said goodbye. 'I have to go out for a bit', I smiled and went out.

31. Kan

The atmosphere at work was tense when Kan deliberately avoided me. During lunchtime, he also disappeared.

A colleague asked, 'What's wrong with him? I haven't heard him curse anyone since this morning.' Another voice chimed in, 'This is a big change. Or has he met a formidable opponent?'. Then came a series of other scattered, sarcastic comments.

'Or maybe he's in love!'. The last sentence ended the scrutiny. They quickly agreed to that theory. They ate and drank, reassured by the idea that love was the key to all mood changes.

That was what they thought; my thinking was different. Unhappiness or happiness might not come from love; why couldn't someone just say outright that it was because of lust and desire?

I called Kan. But his phone was turned off.

While munching on my cake, I went to the record centre. I wanted to buy some new films. I ran into Kan there.

We silently selected the tapes, not saying a word to each other. Kan's face was cold. I kept sneaking glances at him. Ten minutes passed, and we still kept a quiet distance. But my heart fluttered.

We slept together one night ago.

32. camera

The light was dim, dipped in warm yellow. Two bodies pressed together on the sofa, clothes slowly removed. One arm wrapped around the other's neck and then stroked along the back and down the buttocks. The two heads tilted, changing directions continuously. Their lips stuck together.

A head slid down the neck, chest, belly, and down, down again, and then stopped at the junction. The other person's legs were raised high, wide, and the neck was stretched. Underneath, the lowered head had found a core of hot flesh to fill its longing.

The room was filled with sensual sounds. The salon emitted steam.

They moved toward the bed, the last piece of cloth slipping down. They clung to each other. The dark light pooled in the crevice of the dorsal surface. There were two moving bodies and continuously morphing curves. The layout couldn't have been more complete.

On the ceiling hung a giant fish skeleton. The bones cut the nightlight into arcs, and then rotated, crisscrossing each other, forming countless small diamond-shaped cells. They covered two naked bodies like a hood.

In that light, two fish stretched their fins side by side, breathing heavily. Their skin was wet.

33. The devil's childhood

'I don't believe in God, nor do I believe in the Buddha.'

'So what do you believe in?'

'I believe in devils.'

'Devils? Are you kidding? Why?'

'Because they're close to humans. They belong to me. They used to be in me. I believe in each of us there is a germ of a demon; they're lurking somewhere, like the corpses of lice, waiting for the right moment to come back to life, burrowing straight into the place where they taste blood.'

'That is unconvincing. But in your case, did you find a way to control it? How many times has it arisen in you?'

'I don't know. Once or twice. Maybe more. But maybe it was me a long time ago, taking over me completely.'

'Tell me some of your memories.'

'What do you want to hear?'

'Whatever. Let's talk about your childhood, for example.'

'Childhood? My childhood was a series of days behind locked doors, waiting. At first I waited for my father, and then I wasn't sure what I was waiting for. Maybe I needed an incident. Many times I wished the house would catch on fire, so that I would try my best to climb through that locked door. It's stupid. But nothing happened. My childhood was trapped, locked behind such desires.'

'Why were you waiting for your father? Where did he go? Did he work far from home?'

'I don't know. My parents were divorced. My father sometimes visited me and my mother, shoving a cake in my hand. To this day, I don't remember the exact colour, shape, or flavour of that cake. I don't know if it was good. He left nothing specific in my memory, other than a piece of cake. I threw away the cake soon afterwards; I didn't want to eat it. And because I didn't eat it, I don't remember how he looked like either. I don't have any warm feelings towards him.'

'How old were you then? Did your parents explain why they broke up?'

'I don't know. They didn't beat each other, at least in my view. Sometimes they argued. I was about seven years old then. One afternoon, the teacher had a personal matter, so she let the class leave early. Instead of waiting for my father to pick me up, I climbed onto the back of the gym teacher's bicycle and hitched a ride. I hurried home, intending to make my father happy because he didn't have to waste time coming to pick me up. I thought of the cassava cake that my mother would give me for my perfect grade in writing.

'But when I entered the house, I saw my mother crying while she was cooking. There was no one in the living room. When I asked her what had happened, she didn't answer but cried even louder. She said that, from then on, we had to learn to take care of each other; from then on, our family had only two people. I wasn't old enough to ask more meaningful questions. Probably because of this, my mother didn't find it necessary to disclose the reason why they broke up.

'Over time, I got used to the situation, got used to the way of thinking that, if a father abandons a child, it's not necessary to ask why or to even look for him. Finding someone is an adult's job; if they end a relationship, it's their responsibility to mend the broken pieces, not mine. People should accept the loss in the same way as they accept being late or getting on the wrong train. If they try to fix it, they will have to go somewhere else entirely; the return trip would take a lot of time. Since I was a passive creature, I needed to practice forgetting. I forgot him like I forgot the cake I threw away.'

'Then what? Did you ever see him again?'

'No. He just faded away and disappeared. He left with no pain, no regrets, nor remorse. Like a car passing in front of us, he vanished in a thin swirl of dust, dissolving into the air. We moved to another place. I took the bus by myself after school, went home, showered myself, and watched TV alone. I remember at that time there was no colour TV. The world seen through a black-and-white screen forced me to enhance my ability to relate to reality and to magnify my imagination. Sometimes I was satisfied with the different view, like how the sun was not only orange or red, the forest was not just green, cows were not always golden brown—they could be grey like the way black-and-white televisions are. Or it could suddenly fade away if I wasn't in a good mood that day. In general, it depended on my own perspective. After that, when my mother came home from work, we would quietly eat dinner together.

'I never saw my father again. My mother stopped

crying in the kitchen; she turned into an irritable woman. When I did something against her will, she scolded me severely, and even threw vegetables in my face. If I got bad grades, she swore at me, saying I was useless and stupid. Over time, I no longer needed to share my thoughts with her. I kept them as my own. Sometimes, in retrospect, I'm grateful to her. Thanks to that harsh, somewhat abusive upbringing, I became strong. I learned to solve problems on my own, one by one. Each year I became more confident. I decided not to disturb her as my mother, other than to ask her to go to a parent-teacher conference twice a year. I became the best in my class, my health was excellent, my conduct was impeccable, and I was always good. Twice a year, my mother had the opportunity to smile proudly for me. She stopped throwing things at me or cursing me for being stupid. But she was still cranky. She turned to attack our neighbours. She immediately turned on anyone who simply hinted at her past.'

'Perhaps your mother was lost after the divorce. It could also be due to the psychological stress that came from hard work. She couldn't control herself.'

'Yeah, maybe. But she did a lot of scary, even evil things.'

'Why do you make such harsh comments about your mother?'

'Because I once saw her poison a neighbour's cat when

it stole a fish from our kitchen. When she was done, she carried the cat's body out to the gate of its owner's house, skewered on a sharp stake, with a note attached: "Pay back my fish with death!"

'I shrank and asked my mother, "Why did the cat have to pay such a high price?" My mother said, "You're still very young, you don't understand anything. Since your father left, our family's economic situation has become worse. In a week, we can only eat one meal of fish. The rest are vegetables, ketchup and only a few tiny eggs. There will never be any slice of meat. So it isn't acceptable for a cat to steal the only fish in the week. We don't get to eat it, but the neighbour's cat enjoyed eating it; don't you think that's unfair, Kan?"

'I asked again, "But why did it cost its life?" It had to pay—my mother insisted—because she didn't want this to happen again. Therefore, more than simply killing, it was a warning. "It's to restore order, to seek justice. Kan, do you understand? Now follow me, toughen up, hide in that fence, and watch what happens next."

'Honestly, at that time, my brain was almost frozen, bewildered; as if hypnotised, I followed my mother's instructions. Behind the fence, I waited. To this day, I still can't forget the horrified look on my neighbour's face; she almost froze to death with her eyes wide open. It looked as if she had been momentarily paralysed all over, as if she were clinically dead. I daresay that, in the horror films I watched later in life, there has been no scene that shocked me like that. Really. I'm not exaggerating.

'But looking at that scene, I couldn't help but enjoy it. I burst out laughing. And then in a sort of chain effect, I found the cat's pathetic look very funny. Its eyes, pale yellow and glittering in the sky, showed the same terror as its owner. I laughed nonstop. For the first time, I discovered the joy of childhood, which was to see others in awe of something. After that event, I gradually discovered that I began to live with evil.'

'What else do you do after that? Something evil?'

'Something evil? Countless to tell! After a while, the story about the cat spread all throughout the neighbourhood, and then somehow my schoolmates caught wind of it. I was ostracised. I guess someone in the neighbourhood had a hand in it. Unfortunately, there were two boys and a girl who were in the same school as my neighbours. I tried to track down who the culprit was but to no avail. But at school, I became more and more isolated. I got caught up in petty conflicts, and couldn't ask my mother for help. I had to conceal the bruises and wash my own clothes of the blood and dirt that came from the fights before my mother found out. I had to make up excuses. Of course, sometimes, I had to endure my mother's beatings, leaving my body bruised and worn out, which was way worse than fighting with my friends. As I said, I had to learn to defend myself and deal with my own personal problems.'

'Did you always have to push yourself like that?'

'Push myself? Of course! But as a child, I didn't really understand that. I thought I was having a normal life—that it was a natural way to cope, like the way an eel emits electricity, a hedgehog ruffles its quills or some plants have their venom: there's a reason for all of that. If you don't have anyone reliable around you, then you must learn to protect yourself and overcome all obstacles by yourself. If you survive, you've done well. But really, I've grown up, survived and am lying next to you. So I was right, wasn't I?'

'Yes, true to a certain extent. Every child needs to be protected.'

'Of course, but sometimes it's necessary to leave them alone, toss them out in the street to give them some encouragement. Let me tell you: I almost killed a bastard in my class once.'

'Why?'

'Because he said I looked like a wild dog. I challenged him, "Say it again". He shouted, "I said you're a wild dog, okay?" "That means a dirty and uneducated bastard? You want to put it exactly like that, don't you?" I asked calmly. He nodded, cocking his head, smiling proudly. A crowd had gathered in a circle to watch us. I could read the desire in the bloodshot eyes of those savages, who were craving a fight. Okay, I would satisfy them all. I put all my strength and the inhibitions that had accumulated over the years into my hands, and rushed to strangle that bastard. The circle around us cheered, "Go on, go on!". They chanted rhythmically, their footsteps followed our movements; their dance was like a ritual, like foxes dancing in a cave, celebrating a successful hunt. My heart rate soared. Each time they chanted "go on", my arms squeezed a little tighter. The boy's breath was wheezing. His throat heaved with loud hiccups, and then he passed out. At first he struggled, but then he didn't fight any more. He let go of his arms and legs. I strangled him until he rolled his eyes, tongue sticking out, unable to breathe. I assumed he was dead, and I was about to let out a sigh of relief.

'Suddenly, the circle stopped cheering. An eerie silence prevailed. And then suddenly the ground shook; the circle broke. They scattered and fled, screaming for help. At the time, I didn't know what had happened; something terrible must have happened to make that delighted crowd run away. I let go of the boy's neck. He fell to the ground and lay flat on the grass. At that time,

I remembered the cat that stole the fish and paid with its death on a spike, with a warning note attached. I thought the guy was dead. So I rummaged through my bag, pulled out a piece of paper, and thought about how to make a poignant statement, just like my mother did. Then I imagined how the motherfucker's mother would also be so stunned as she read the piece of paper pinned on her child's body. Oh, the emotion rose up in me as strongly as the time when I witnessed my neighbour's expression. When I finished writing the words: "A word of anger, stop breathing forever", with an arrow pointing downwards, I planned to stick the piece of paper on his forehead.

'But by the time I looked up, he had already run away. I didn't chase after him. To this day, I still don't understand why I didn't. Something welled up in my eyes, wet and cold, but I swear they weren't tears. How could I believe I was crying when I'd just put all my energy into killing my enemy? What was there to cry about? Was it really necessary to cry? Was I crying out of regret? Or was I crying because he came back to life, which meant I would be free from attempted murder? Or did I cry because I was afraid of myself? No! They were absolutely not tears. Maybe it was because I was fighting so hard that my eyelids sweat. Well, it was only then that I felt my legs droop. My shaking hands tightened into fists. I crumpled the piece of paper and swallowed it.'

'Oh my gosh—then what? The school must have handled this very well?'

'Not at all! No one said a thing. The teachers didn't know anything since no one dared to rat on me, probably because they were afraid of the backlash. Since then, the whole class was afraid of me. The demon inside me shouted for victory; it saved me from the torment of the crowd. Therefore, I was determined to nurture it, without a doubt, expecting it to grow day by day. I learned the truth: To win, you must know cruelty.'

'For all these years, have you just solved all problems with violence?'

'Not really. In many cases, I realised that violence was synonymous with defeat, if I were to meet a stronger opponent. I then switched to using tactics. I marked that milestone at the age of twelve, at the beginning of puberty.'

'So early? It wasn't until I was fourteen that I had my first wet dream.'

'That's too bad you took so long to mature. But look at you now—you're fine, aren't you?'

'In order to catch up, I had to make up for two more years as compared to you.'

'Yeah, where was I?'

'Twelve years old, puberty, you switched to using tactics.'

'That's right. That's when I met a stronger opponent. This guy was in another class, bigger than me. Perhaps because the incident reached his ears, he was eager to compete with me. Kids are aggressive and noisy, you know that. Any brat would think that he was endowed with some kind of incomparable, absolute power. In need of confirmation, they are eager to test that strength. And this big guy was really good at sniffing out potential prey. At recess, when he passed through the window, scanning me sideways, I knew immediately what was going to happen. He knew who would be his prey. I tried to calm myself down. But I didn't expect the contest to take place so soon, in a place where I was completely caught off guard: in the bathroom. Yes, as soon as I opened the zippers of my pants in the toilet, he punched me; I ran away with a mouth full of blood. One of my teeth was broken; my lips spread out. He chased me around the schoolyard. I took refuge in the supervisor's room and was safe for a while before coming back to my class.'

'He didn't stop there? Was he going to find you to finish you off?'

'Correct! I could tell from my experience. Therefore, instead of passively waiting for him to strike, I wanted to prepare a weapon for a counter-attack. The question was what weapon to find. During the remaining two classes, I sat frozen in my chair, not listening, not understanding what the teacher was saying, my mind reeling with the prospect of being attacked. I thought maybe I'd be beaten to death, and my pitifully crumpled body would then be hung on the school fence, or torn in front of my gate. The image of the dead cat that stole the fish suddenly came to mind. Its exposed body haunted me. I didn't want to die. I never wanted my mother to freeze up, standing there like our neighbour. I kept looking at the board. The teacher was writing, her hand went up and down rhythmically, the chalk dust kept falling, white as snow. I blinked, ecstatic. Ah, I got it! The chalk dust—thank you!'

'Chalk dust? What for?'

'To counter his attack. As expected, when I walked out of the school gate, I saw the guy with the steel fist standing proudly in the distance, shirtless like an outstanding boxer. He smiled radiantly. Behind him there was a crowd of spectators, cheering. Why couldn't this mob of barbarians let go of me? They were afraid of me, but they never let me go. I proudly looked my foe straight in the eye, walked over, and clenched my fists. Only I knew what was in my hand. At an appropriate distance, my opponent threw a punch. Just in time, I also released both my fists, aiming it straight in his face. Everything was white and hazy.

His head was like a piece of breaded meat. The bastard screamed in terror, covered his face with his hands, and rubbed it. Chalk dust! I thought he must've been blind. There was so much chalk dust. He could've spent his life punching the air with those blind eyes.'

'Oh my God, that's terrible!'

"Yes, the surrounding crowd also said so. What a coincidence! But I see nothing terrible here. I was just defending myself. No one taught me a better way to defend myself, so I had to figure it out on my own. Why didn't anyone teach them not to fight with me? I wouldn't take revenge if I wasn't bullied in the first place. So who was at fault here? And which side needs to be taught first in order to have peace? Either way, I'm glad I won. Yes, I always win. I win because I know how to teach myself.'

'How did it end? How about that poor boy's eyes?'

'What? You say poor boy? That's just pathetic. After all, that stupid thug, he wasn't blind; dust couldn't have made him blind. He just had to go to the doctor and miss school for two days—everything was fine. After he came back to school, he kept staring at me without blinking. I understood that look. Fear and hatred. Then he would be like me: to overcome fear, he could only use hatred as his motivation to create his strength. No one knew when hatred would overcome fear. That day, I threw chalk dust into his eyes; one day he might throw coal ashes, paprika, sand, or some goddamn thing into my eyes, how would I know? An endless game of hatred, you know? I was restless. My student life at that time was a living hell. It was only when I got home that I was fine, as I knew that I still had a chance to survive. The heavy burden of that day left me exhausted. It wasn't until he suddenly transferred to another school that I felt revived. I also don't know if he transferred schools due to his personal circumstances or because he wanted to avoid confrontation with me. Anyway, I was exhausted from worrying for a long time. You see: between me and him, who's more pitiful?'

***

It was almost morning; I could hear Kan's regular breaths. My arms were numb. Kan's head was resting on my arm. 'Sleep soundly, Kan.' I wished that his childhood hadn't been like that. I wished that Kan hadn't thrown away the cake his father gave him, so that he would still have some memory of his father. I wished Kan had been taught how to survive without fighting, so that he wouldn't be too proud to live with the motto 'I teach myself how to survive' without being lost because of his pain. I wished that Kan could believe that the tears that come after you kill someone are real.

Yes, in this case Kan was indeed pitiful. But what about me? Between me and Kan, who was more pitiful?

The dawn had already come, and I missed G.g.

34. calculating

I was afraid of the new day. I'd been hanging around the house for a whole month. H didn't come last night. If H doesn't come, the night doesn't mean anything to me.

I looked at the painting *Dancing in the Shower* on the wall, wondering why I used grey to paint them. That layer of grey, like dew, made me unable to distinguish what was water and what was mist in the shower.

H once asked the reason why I did so; I just made a joke, 'So you want the other body to be completely naked?'

He retorted, 'The person is taking a shower, why can't he be naked?'

I protested, 'Look, it's a genderless body. The blur makes it more emotional.'

'More speculation. The boundaries are not so clear when the brush strokes and sieving techniques have made everything so blurry. Do you accept this interpretation?' asked H.

'Oh, right. You're always better at expressing things than I am.'

I thought H really liked this painting. He encouraged me to draw a whole set of three to five paintings of the same theme. When mushrooms withered and the viper plant bloomed with purple flowers, I would hang this set of paintings on the long wall leading from the living room to the stairs. The sombre walls not only breathed and danced, they also helped to turn the house into an exceptional gallery.

H placed his hand on the wall as if he were touching imaginary paintings. At the bottom of his eyes, there was a hint of happiness. He turned, walked backwards, moved upstairs step by step, muttering 'Here, here...' and then stopped, one foot dangling into the air as if preparing to fly.

'Great. You will study more angles. But you shouldn't get bogged down in a tight layout forever. I find that sometimes the skewed lines will give you more inspiration for deduction.'

Deductive inspiration—he had a special way of pairing words. I thought H had a point. Okay, I was going to do a five-part study of genderless humans bathing. But was it necessary to always use moss-grey tones?

I told H that I needed a model, and H said, 'It's up to you. I can't do it for you. My body has many flaws; it doesn't look good at all.'

'Come on H. You have to love your body. If you don't know how to love yourself, who else can you love?'

'If you love yourself too much, you'll become a narcissist, G.g.'

'Please stop spouting nonsense. By the way, would you be willing to take off your clothes for me to study your body?'

'G.g, I beg you. In the daylight, I'm not confident enough.'

I burst out laughing. Why was this brave man in the dark so afraid to expose his body to the light? Did he expose it to me, the one he once hugged and bonded with?

'Why's that, H? What's the problem here? What has made you feel so ashamed? We are one; we belong together. Do you think I'm a mirror? Do I make you ashamed when you look at me? Fine, then, if you don't have the courage to model for me, introduce me to someone else. Or do I find someone myself? Don't think that I'm crazy. I desperately need a model. Help me, please.'

35. doubt

During that time, I felt insecure. For several days, I considered G.g.'s suggestion. He asked me to help him find a male model, but I was apprehensive. As a slave of my own imagination, I endlessly weaved an enchanting vision that took place in G.g.'s studio, where only the two were entwined. Would they just work cooperatively? Where are the limits? What would motivate G.g to go through the steps without breaking away from temptation?

I thought of Kan. After the night we slept together, I understood many things. At any moment in life, everyone could slip into decadence and indulge in erotic games. Whether that game ends early or keeps us stuck, no one can say for sure. I started the game, and G.g would play that game too.

What should I do to stop that game?

36. albino cemetery

One morning G.g. said we couldn't continue playing the games of drowning the sun, torturing objects to paralysis, disguising poisonous mushrooms, or scaring an orphaned wolf forever. We absolutely needed a new game.

'We need to come up with something!' I threw the

blanket off and jumped up, pulling on my underwear.

We took a knife and went out into the garden. It was wet with dew. G.g looked around, and said, 'We need to reorganise this garden.' I added, 'You have to give it a special touch.' 'Something barbaric,' G.g finished, flicking his knife across a tree branch that blocked his view.

We had knives in hand, our eyes darting around and thinking. 'Something barbaric'. Yes—this idea drove us both crazy.

While we were searching on the other side of the fence, a voice said, 'They're starting to kill again. It's disgusting!'

Bang! The tip of the knife flew from G.g's hand and crashed straight into the wall where the voice came from, slicing a vine branch. The voice on the other side of the fence fell silent.

'Run! The madman will kill us!' The wild screams tore through the morning mist, followed by panicked footsteps stepping on the branches. The crackling echoes receded, restoring a momentary silence to the garden. Early morning sunlight penetrated the canopy of leaves. The bush stopped flowering because it could sense something dangerous. A few squeaky barks from the wolf cub standing on the steps rose up here and there.

'Humph, nasty neighbours. I had to give them a

warning to scare them off. Next time I come across those brats, I'll definitely cut them open.'

'Like dissecting a bitter melon', I chimed in and laughed out loud. I suddenly remembered G.g's description of bitter melon soup stuffed with the dreaded wood ear mushroom. I felt nauseous.

It was a morning that promised to be filled with excitement. The game was about to begin.

G.g led me to the mound at the end of the garden, where there was a plant I didn't know the name of. It was a mixture of eucalyptus and willow, its mouldy bark peeling off in dry, curved white patches like a body with tinea versicolour. There was also a cluster of sharp, dark purple needles around the soft branches. G.g said that the plant only bloomed once every seven years, and only bore red flowers on rainy and windy days. When there was no rain, the flowers immediately bloomed with white spots and then shrivelled on the branches, right in the middle of the tip of the needle cluster. I had never heard of a plant with such monstrous properties, and couldn't imagine the scene when it bloomed. I felt nervous. When I touched the tree trunk, a piece of bark fell off, revealing a thin layer of silk covered with white dust.

G.g said, 'You name it. When I moved to live here, I saw it standing there. I've wanted to kill it for a long time. Evil needles. Once I was stung by its needles when I accidentally bumped into it. Honestly, I'm curious—I'll have to wait and see how it blooms anyway.'

'Haven't you seen its flowers?' I asked in surprise. 'Who described it to you?'

'A neighbour of mine. They say it's not unusual for these plants; they used to grow around here. The neighbour doesn't know its name either. I don't understand why they've gradually died over time. Some of them, instead of blooming red flowers, simultaneously bloomed white flowers as if they were mourning. People are afraid of bad luck, so they cut them down.'

My spine went numb, as if I were shocked by a jolt of electricity. I took a few steps back, looking closely at the branches and leaves waving in the wind, like hundreds of feathers reaching out to grab me. Pieces of bark peeled off, exposing the tree's guts, giving me an image of a fleshy body. It stood there, wriggling its limbs in the wind like it was crying out in frustration. My hand trembled, 'Why leave it in the garden? What's the point?' I asked.

'I'm just waiting for it to flower. Simple as that. Come on, give it a name.'

We stood thinking for a long time. I found this game silly. I wasn't interested, nor could I think of a name for it. The sun was high in the sky; it was getting hotter and hotter. I said, 'A needle tree?'

'Not good', G.g countered. 'Look at its bark; it looks like it's rotten. So let's call it an albino tree.'

I felt tired and dizzy; my eyes widened and I simply nodded to end the game. Yes, the albino tree. I went back into the house. I remembered that the two of us had not eaten anything this morning. I was about to collapse from hunger.

G.g stopped me. He pointed to the stump. 'In a year I will kill the lovely wolf and bury it under this tree. So please help me design an impressive stele. I don't know what to say on the tombstone. Maybe the line, 'The resting place of the short-lived orphan wolf' should work. Poor little creature. It will die without being called a dog as it should have been. But it has to die. What do you think?'

I didn't think at all. I was tired of trying to figure out why the dog was forced to die. I just wanted to go indoors, so I nodded in response to whatever G.g said.

'That's not all. When I make that grave here, this mound will look morbid. Imagine, on rainy and windy nights, bunches of red flowers will bloom and fall, decorating the wolf's grave. Well, there's no horror film that's as tragic as this. I'll put the cameras here and there too. Great! Let's see, then, we'll call this the wolf cemetery. Oh no—the albino mound. No, let's think about it a little more; the wolf will be fried in a pan of oil. Surely its skin would peel off dry and crispy, just like this tree bark. All right, let's call it the albino cemetery.'

Albino cemetery? No problem. I'd save the poor wolf cub and burn this damn tree for sure.

37. the owl's eyes

G.g asked me to buy cigarettes and kerosene. He was busy drawing. Because the gas station was quite far away, I decided to go to a grocery store in the neighbourhood, hoping to get what I needed.

On my return, I passed a house with an old, heavy iron gate, and a small, quiet garden lined with trees. In the middle of the gate, about halfway up, there was a rather large owl-shaped relief. It was only then that I took notice of the house. I walked slowly as I watched the owl. The black copper-plated owl, revealing mossy green sores and big bulging eyes, looked at me like a stalker. The owl's deep eyes swallowed the quiet atmosphere that was trying to expand. It exuded tremendous power, pulling me closer to the gate. It reminded me of the dead cat's eyes in Kan's childhood story. The owl made me want to touch it.

'Murderer. What are you going to do?'

I withdrew my hand. Beneath the owl's eyes, a pair of human eyes suddenly appeared. There was a boy—I couldn't guess his age—who was wearing a grey shirt, clutching his hand to the gate. His irises were motionless, his glare more terrifying than the owl's, piercing my flesh like sharp shards of a broken glass bottle.

'Bastard, what did you say? Who's the murderer?' I flared up, with a hint of discomfort.

'It's you. Why did you kill my puppies? At night, they'd just lost their way while walking for a while. They were innocent. It's my fault that I forgot to close the gate. Why did you kill them?'

'It wasn't me. Are you crazy? I don't live here, I'm just a visitor. I've just met you for the first time. I haven't seen anything here yet. How could I know your puppies?' I realised that my voice came out as monotonous as a machine, with an unnecessary air of sincerity.

'I know you did it. You erased every single trace. Too bad I didn't catch you doing it', his voice was sharp. He gulped, kept his sharp gaze, and then, with an air of sarcasm, continued, 'But hey, let it go. They're gone anyway.'

'Slanderer! I'm going to break your neck', I said, unable

to bear his smugness.

'What terrible words. I'm not mistaken; I have seen you carry a knife to kill and slaughter all over the garden. Isn't your house over there?' He jerked his jaws towards G.g.'s wooden house.

Ah, so that's it. He was likely one of those guys who screamed and ran away one morning when G.g and I were wandering the albino mound. I suddenly remembered the story of the thirteen wolves; did G.g really kill them? This kid was accusing me now, and his argument was solid. Perhaps he had confused me with G.g?

'You think so? But why aren't you afraid of me now?' I lowered my voice.

'Why be afraid?'

We were facing each other through the gate, and I almost touched him. I didn't even know if I wanted to grab him or not. He remained unchanged in both his gaze and posture, his pale blue veins pulsing under the skin. His skin was a surreal shade of white, almost transparent.

'Didn't you bring a knife today? I have never seen anyone with such a big knife, like a sword. How can you carry something that dangerous on your shoulders without falling?'

'What? Can you speak normally?' I was shocked, my eyes widening in astonishment. He looked like a monster.

'Come on, what makes you think I'm abnormal? I make you feel threatened, don't I?'

God, my arms were so numb. My jaw and my tongue were frozen. At this point, I was sure that he wasn't a demon-possessed creature, but had actually become a demon. I tried to control the anger rising up in my throat. I struggled to make a sound, hearing my voice just flow through the broken, distorted tip of my tongue, 'Look at the way you talk: *carrying something that dangerous on your shoulders... make you feel threatened.* Who taught you to talk like that, little devil?'

'Anger has bogged you down. Don't you realise I'm not a kid? I'll tell you: I'm twenty or so. The language I've used with you has been very appropriate, and the expression has also been perfectly precise and clear.'

The language I've used with you, precise and clear, oh my, I was afraid I'd have a stroke. I wasn't sure what world I was in. I didn't believe the kid in front of me was real at all. What planet did he come from? An alternate world? Hell? Or something similar. What did he just say? Was he about twenty years old? That chubby face? Maybe he was crazy.

The owl, the masterful predator, looked at me mockingly. My hand was cold. It was my turn to stand still while the boy changed positions, his legs and arms crossed in a very insolent way. It felt like I was the one standing inside the fence, a criminal locked in a prison, and that little demon was the executioner who was performing the interrogation. He and the owl were attacking me. I was about to be butchered.

'Ha ha ha...' he burst out laughing. The sky swayed with his laughter. I was drained and dizzy; my chest tightened. It felt like I was an inflated plastic dummy that had just been pierced by the echoing laughter, drained of air, and in a moment my body would collapse into a completely useless mass. I tried to stand upright, resting my feet against the gate. Suddenly there was a call from the house that sounded like an old man's voice.

He slowly took a few steps back, looked at me, and smiled confusedly. Before running away, he whispered, 'Look at you! Don't be afraid, it's no more than just a game. Let's just say I'm rehearsing a play. But I know quite well who you are. Hey, murderer, you're my neighbour. Do you like the owl? Touch it. Kiss it. Be brave. Let's relax. See you later. Goodbye.'

He disappeared in a flash. I swore that in the time he spoke until he ran away, I didn't blink once. He didn't run into the house, so where did he go? It looked like he disappeared into thin air. I saw it with my own eyes. Unbelievable. The sunlit wall swallowed him up. He really was a devil.

The owl kept its eyes open, glaring at its prey. It seemed to fall on my head. I collapsed by the iron gate before I could kiss it.

38. the voices on the other side of the fence

I asked H, 'Where have you been for so long? Why are my clothes dusty and covered with green moss?'

H didn't answer. With a grey face, he staggered to the red sofa and collapsed. I knew he didn't like the red sofa—what had happened? I shook him, but he didn't move. He didn't explain anything.

I left him there.

I visited the albino cemetery, trying to figure out how the wolf stele would be designed.

On the other side of the fence, mixed with the wind, were human voices, almost like children's voices. I strained my ears to catch them. A vague voice filled with provocative mockery, 'It's the killer. Shh! See what he does.'

Those nasty kids again. My head was on fire. Why couldn't they leave me alone? I thought to myself, if I caught them, I'd cut them into thin slices. Then they would be found in the form of a steak.

My heart was broken. I savoured the feeling of pleasure for a long time to let it soak into my blood vessels, and then I stood on tiptoe to approach the fence, trying to hear something on the other side. I couldn't get over this fence without a ladder. But at the moment I didn't have a ladder. I regretted not bringing a knife.

I decided to throw an imaginary knife into the air, through the wall. On the other side, the human voice suddenly stopped. On this side, the wind was still gently blowing through the albino trees.

39. beauty is darkness

That was Kan's definition.

Everyone was startled when they heard Kan's response to a customer who preferred elegant, bright colours. However, Kan's design, even after being revised for the third time, still couldn't convince the customer who always scoffed at the colour schemes. To be fair, I found the drawing acceptable; one of the three was indeed quite nice. But it was difficult to predict what others wanted.

Perhaps because he was too exasperated, Kan immediately smeared the design, changed the colour tone to black, grey and brown, and then threw it in the customer's face. Casually watching the shock that had not yet dissipated on the customer's face, Kan also added, 'I advise you to change your perception of colour. I know exactly the kind of client you are: people who are too proud with little knowledge of what you want. You really don't know what you want, do you? You also clearly don't know what is beautiful. So, listen carefully. Beauty is darkness. LIKE THIS!' Kan vented his frustration with each stressed word, and at the same time, pointed his index finger at the darkest area on the drawing, his lips raised in defiance; his eyebrows twitched slightly and triumphantly.

Consequences: the customer went away and never returned.

The colleagues laughed hysterically and Kan pretended to be calm, ready to accept the boss's wrath. Fear was raging inside him, I guessed, even though on the surface he was trying to fit into his calm coat.

Ultimately, there were no closed-door meetings that day.

It didn't rain that afternoon, but Kan stayed over and refused to come back after his shift. Even after all our colleagues had already left, he just sat still, his face fossilised. I remembered how he had been the last time. I was scared.

I went to cut off the power. Kan still didn't budge. In the reflected light, I saw the statue of Kan shining with perfect lines and beauty. 'Beauty is darkness.' I thought that he was right. I carefully locked the door and hugged him for a long time. He didn't resist. My lips melted into the nape of his neck, my breath entering his mouth. I wished that we could be one forever.

After the kiss, I wanted to take him home like last time. I wanted to sleep with him again, again and again. I couldn't resist the desire that was straining intensely in my crotch.

40. cockroach circus, sea blood, silent call

G.g talked over the phone, his voice urgent. 'Help me. They're crawling everywhere; they're going to attack me. There're hundreds of them.'

'What is it, G.g? It's two in the morning, don't you know?'

'Cockroaches! They're crawling all over the floor; they're swinging on wires, sliding down from the gap in the windows.'

'Calm down, please. Where's the insect repellent?'

'I don't know. How do I kill them all? Why do they hide their faces during the day, but show up at night? Do they come from the night?'

I yawned away from the phone. Beside me, Kan turned his body. He pulled the blanket over his bare bottom as he rearranged his legs to keep himself warm, grumbling, 'You should sleep... Who are you talking to at this hour?'

I bent down to kiss Kan's forehead, whispering, 'Never mind. Someone is asking for my advice.' I crawled out of bed, not forgetting to give him a deceitful wink.

Once I had settled into the living room salon, I began to hear what G.g had to say. He recounted every detail as if the cockroaches were monsters. I was sick of him. Just like the night he killed the wolves, I thought he might've been haunted. Maybe there were only five or six cockroaches, or a few more, but he always made matters worse and multiplied them into the hundreds and thousands. I knew that he was sloppy; he rarely cleaned the house, but the wooden house had not yet become a garbage dump.

'What have they done?' I tried to sound worried.

'They're waiting. I just gave them some bread crumbs. They refuse to go away. They're crawling around, huddled together to plan something. They're jumping on each other's backs. I don't dare to stick my feet out of the bed. Tell me how? It's disgusting—I'm going to die.'

'There has never been a case of cockroaches eating humans, except for corpses. G.g., listen. One: find the repellent spray right away. Two: grab a few; drop them in the toilet and flush. The rest will automatically retreat after seeing you do that. Can you hear me?'

'Where do I grab them?'

'Their antennae. Or turn them upside down on the floor. That's how to disable cockroaches; their legs will wave towards the sky and twitch, looking very funny. Try it and see. They will wait and die a humiliating, irreparable death.'

'Really? I'll go do it right now. I'll call you back later.'

G.g kissed me through the phone. I put it down. Hopefully Kan didn't hear anything. I went back to Kan's side, and of course he was still asleep. I wanted to lie down and hug him—so peaceful and warm—but I was afraid that G.g would call me back. So I went back to the living room and sat down on my knees, sullen, waiting. That was it: a sweet night simply stolen by G.g.

I just sat there. I didn't know for how long. At first, I was annoyed. I thought, slowly but surely, G.g and I were drifting apart just because of phone calls at wrong times like this. In the darkness that surrounded me, I tried to remember all the relationships I've had and lost. In those many relationships, there were some things that I treasured, like trust, sincerity, pure kindness, for example. Whenever I broke up with someone, I was often too occupied, so I didn't have time to calm down to analyse why it came to an end.

Then, like in a law of equilibrium, when one relationship disappeared, another immediately came to me. They were certainly different. A new relationship, however, could never fill the void in me. It wouldn't be fair to say that I didn't suffer any loss—but I didn't seem to fully comprehend the sense of the word. The invisible void expanded over time. In another moment, I'd lose control. And it either exploded like a ticking time bomb, leaving me with a deep black hole, or it would harden and dive into the recesses deep within me, turning into a benign tumour. All my life, I've lived with such tumours without knowing it. I didn't even feel like I was sick. But in the end, the tumours invaded good places in my body and mind; they always destroyed beautiful, healthy cells. They suddenly mutated into malignant tumours. In other words, they were the dark phantoms at the bottom of my soul: incurable cancers.

Putting aside all the distractions of reality, I let my thoughts settle down while waiting for G.g.'s phone call.

It was an endless stretch of time. Flashing back to the distant past, I used to wait for a phone call from a friend, like this.

***

Back then, we were doing an internship together during the first semester of our sophomore year. My friend said that he wanted to sketch fishermen and fishing activities. I preferred the forest. The mountains and forests, crowded with murky, overlapping layers of trees, always gave me endless inspiration. Our interests were the exact opposites. I didn't know what he had in mind, but he was very eager to study sketches of a poor, sleazy world. I could never explain why. In fact, he was better off than many in our class, almost like a bourgeois. While we went to ballet classes to study the beautiful movements of shapes and lines of human body, or to parks to copy the beauty of flowers and leaves, or to the zoo to paint animals with their beautiful hooves, he was different. From four o'clock in the morning he went on his own to fruit and vegetable markets, popular working-class areas, and busy sidewalk shops to record all activities there. He focused on these aspects of life, trying to convey the hardships and poverty that appeared on every austere and anxious facial expression.

When I first saw his eagerness, I thought he was trying to stand out as someone different. But one of my classmates wasn't convinced, suspecting that maybe he could find a source of cruel pleasure in painting that chaotic world. Like a photojournalist passing through a fire, when everyone was panicking and trying to save people, he tried to cut in; but instead of rescuing the poor victims, he took pictures. He brought them back to the newsroom, and was hailed as a hero for a series of unique, exclusive images. The pictures were printed and released, delivering a powerful message with a shudder of sympathy. And he proudly went on to receive the journalist of the year award for his breakthrough images, his bravery, and his humanitarian spirit. At first he was entangled in a sense of guilt, but as time went on, he pushed aside his conscience for professional advancement. He became addicted. He discovered the truth: wrapped in mourning and deadly danger, there is always beauty. A sudden, unusual beauty. A tragic beauty.

Thus, there formed a chain of conditioned reflexes, a conscious need; instead of being passive like the first time, he went on active pursuits. A person's body fell into the abyss, clothes fluttering. A dog had been run over by a car, its organs viscerally flying all over the place, while its four legs were still soaring through the air with inertia, its eyeballs bulging out all the way in an extreme panic.

A house was shot up into the sky by a tornado; shards of glass flew everywhere, stuck in the body of a child who was holding on to the emergency door. There, he published those works, just as effective as images extracted from action films with special effects. Of course he had the right to argue that the accident happened suddenly, and that in the dire circumstances, he could only witness and do nothing more. He had to give up; he couldn't help but witness and raise his camera. Everyone believed him. It was logical. It was worth sympathising with, even admiring, his courage. No one doubted why he always showed up at the right time. Either he staged, or he stalked. Staged like in a film? It was possible but too costly; a crazy theory. Then he must have stalked. Snooping, delighting in seeing the danger. The right term should have been *hunting*. A predator, to be exact. The public was enthralled by his work. They waited for them to reappear. Haven't seen him publish a new photo for a long time, they asked curiously—why haven't we seen another extraordinary photo of his for so long? They were addicted to consumption, and he was addicted to production. The addiction was logical in itself. His works were moments, victories and historical events. He was an apothecary. He turned into a malignant tumour!

My classmate ended the long monologue. His face was red, puffy, and filled with tension. I woke up. Yeah, could he have turned into a tumour?

I immediately found it relatable to my friend. He painted with great passion, but he showed no sympathy for the characters that appeared in his paintings, which always got the highest scores in class. The vividness of his lines, the right composition, the diverse movements, the contrasting and vibrant shapes, not to mention the variable light combination. He had already achieved too much with sketches that actually only served as records. Of course, no one objected to the amazing results my friend achieved. He had talent and deserved full admiration.

We tried to do what he did, but failed. We weren't calm enough in the face of poverty, squalor and filth. We were forced to be imprisoned in the context, in the world we were working so hard to paint. We quickly gave up. We laboured but never reaped the sweet fruit. The first place in class never belonged to us.

Until the day my friend and I went to an island together.

At the time, I wasn't sure why we were so close. Perhaps it was because of my curiosity and admiration for him, plus a sense of reflection; according to that classmate's analysis, my friend's soul was perhaps as distorted and as sick as the photojournalist that he used as an example. In addition to the eagerness of naïve youth, I decided to test the matter myself by enthusiastically going to the island with him.

On the island, there was no mobile phone signal. We rented a fishing boat and swam out to the reef. I had never seen a coral reef in my life; what I saw in the aquarium in the city was just a dead, lifeless model. The stagnant passages in the aquarium would dwarf in comparison with this wild nature. We tried to swim. A fishing village boy was hired to lead the way.

My friend wanted to explore the reef first. He went diving even without any special vest. It wasn't before long that he was bitten by a sea creature. He rose above the water and screamed. From the boat, I saw a slender scarlet thread swishing to the rhythm of his feet. While he tried to swim to the shore, I watched silently, I didn't even fully understand his cry. I stared blankly. It was spectacular. I had never seen such a beautiful sight. It was a dance of blood in the sea. Yes, in despair, there was always beauty. I panned the camera frantically.

When the little fisherman shouted something in my ear, apparently ordering the boat to return to the island quickly, my friend was dragged onto the deck of the boat, one leg still sticking into the water. He was exhausted from blood loss. At that time, I was willing to tear off the sleeve of his shirt tied to his foot to stop the bleeding. I kept thinking about a four-toed foot. The foot with a toe missing must have looked very funny, like half of a body of a crab with its claws cut off. His foot became a kind of disabled beauty; a destroyed structure. Perhaps from that moment on, he wouldn't wear sandals anymore; instead, he might wear shoes for the rest of his life, in hot summers and in rainy days. An imprisoned foot.

The rest of the days on the island, he didn't complain at all, though his toes were so tightly bound that he couldn't walk normally. Something surreal had taken place in the accident, and in his endurance. I've never had a finger or toe amputated, so I didn't feel his pain. But I was sure I'd scream my lungs out if I were him. Why didn't he whine? Some fishermen looked at the sharp cut, guessing it was because of a sharp piece of moat, but the boy who went with us blamed it on a sea snake. I thought about some aquatic species with the proboscis of an octopus. My friend quietly moved to a corner, opened the camera to check, frowned slightly, and quickly deleted all the archive files. The beauty was ruined, I thought, and I couldn't help but regret it.

We continued to work silently. In two days we would board a ship back to the city. With no mobile network, I grew bored easily. The life of a fishing village appeared in my sketches as lifeless as my soul and as quiet as the afternoons on the island.

I wandered along the coconut trees and went on to the reef. I sat there watching the sun go down to the bottom of the water, waiting for the last beam of the sunset to cut into the deep black basin that was falling, covering it. I watched the blade of light waver for a moment, then disappear like it was dipped in a poison solution. In that moment, only the wind howled, mixed with the sound of the waves crashing against the reef, speaking to the pitch-black darkness.

I felt cold, so I wanted to return, but suddenly realised that I had lost my sense of direction. Overthinking the cruel meaning of taking pictures when my friend was in trouble, I had reached the reef without paying attention to the markings. This place must've been too far from the village. If you simply followed the sand, you could end up in a dead end, a reef, or a cliff—or worse, go around forever. I tried to figure out where I was but soon gave up. I had to watch out for the faint light from the house hidden in the coconut grove in the distance. And then I got lost in the wild woods.

In the darkness of the night, I activated the phone to have some light, waving it overhead and hoping someone would spot me. I didn't expect that the island would be so large, and that it would take me so much strength to return to the village. I tried to run, getting lost deeper and deeper in the wild forest. As soon as I got out, I sank into the sand dunes. I cursed the phone. If there was no signal, how could I notify any rescuers? Besides, I guessed, other than me and my friends, there weren't many mobile phone users on this poor island. To make matters worse, if my friend had turned off his phone, who would I call for help? Soon, the battery ran out and this glimmer of hope vanished. I was surrounded by darkness. In the dark, I was free to think and to regret. I was mad at myself: how could I have got lost? When did I leave the fishing village? Why didn't I learn the path to this reef during the day? Enveloped by darkness, I was lost.

The fishing village boy discovered me. I'd been desperate, stuck in the sand with no phone. He appeared at a fateful time, quiet and understanding.

Returning to the house where I was staying, I received news that my friend had left the island since afternoon. That night, I was troubled by many intrusive thoughts.

Back in class, we ended our friendship in silence, with no explanation.

As expected, he never again wore slippers when he left the house; he carefully hid his amputated foot. He stopped sketching the world of poverty. And I tried to erase that dangerous scene from my mind. I stopped being bothered by the sequence of images that came from the accident. I intended to cultivate a healthy, green new world for my own.

***

At this moment, in the dark of the night, I had to wait for G.g's phone call, forced to listen to the story of the damn cockroaches. Waiting was extremely frustrating and exhausting, like a slow suicide.

On the bed, Kan, with his warm body curled up in the blankets, was calling for my embrace; he needed me to respond. Hot blood blazed under my skin. Why should I sacrifice my need to hear cockroach nonsense, born out of G.g's weird mind? I was forced to wait. If I hung up, would our relationship be severed?

Finally, the phone rang. G.g's voice faltered, 'Done. I just took care of them.'

'In one of the ways I told you to?'

'No. I did it my own way.'

'Tell me!'

'It was a Cockroach Circus.'

'What does that mean? Tell me more.'

'Yes, but let's make it tomorrow. I'm so tired now. I need to sleep, H. Sorry. I want to lie down. I wish I could hug you right now and fall asleep. I miss hair strokes; I love back rubs. But tonight no one's going to do that for me.

Am I dying like a child? By the way, I hear your breathing's irregular; you're sure you don't sleep with anyone but me? Aren't you sleeping with someone else?'

The voice faded and died. I was dumbfounded for a moment; I couldn't escape the feeling that I was inhaling G.g's cold breath through the mobile waves. Darkness devoured me.

41. camera

The shadow held a cockroach, raised it to his face, looked at it, and then dangled it from his mouth as if he was about to bite. The shadow muttered, 'Hey shivering cockroaches, flap your wings with your backs glistening in the lamplight. You look like you're sparkling. Sparkling is an illusion. Only the stars have that beautiful feature. Cockroaches are evil creatures; they don't know how to sparkle. They aren't allowed to sparkle.'

The black shadow took off all his clothes and threw them off indiscriminately. Naked, he crawled on the floor, grabbed the cockroaches and locked them in a glass jar where they danced wildly.

The nude shadow spread his clothes on the floor, and then quickly created a thick paste consisting of paint, linseed oil, and then poured it all over his clothes. The mixture was very thick.

The black shadow bent, flexing his arms, making movements like a circus performer.

The circus went on like this:

One: the shadow reached out and picked up fat cockroaches, spinning them blindly by their antennae, and then threw them directly at the clothes on the floor. The painted cockroach couldn't escape, wiggling its wings in despair and was gradually swallowed by the paint.

Two: the shadow repeated the movements, one after the other, until the last cockroach in the glass jar. The shadow changed the direction of rotation from time to time. If one of them had an antenna cut in the middle, the shadow replaced it by sticking two fingers into its leg. When one struggled too much, the shadow cut off the leg. For each cockroach that landed on the gooey paint, the black shadow recited the chorus, 'No sparkling. No sparkling.'

Three: the shadow sprinkled a new layer of paint on the messy surface of the cockroach carcasses and threw the dull brush in there too. Then the cockroach circus painting was completed.

The shadow stood up, whispering, 'I'll hang this special work on the wall. Coated with paint, hundreds of cockroaches will know how to sparkle. Anything covered with acrylic paint has a shine. But no one will expect that the beautiful painting would hide the rotten bodies of evil cockroaches, like this one.'

And the night light suddenly went out. There was no glimmer of light; the shadow was invisible.

42. walking out with Truman Capote

We were sprawled on the attic of the wooden house, watching a film about Truman Capote. This was the first film that G.g watched other than *Farewell My Concubine* since the suicide of Leslie Cheung.

We left the two windows open. Outside, the sun was shining brightly; the wind was blowing through the vines. The cool breeze brought the gentle taste of early autumn from the North. The rain didn't stop completely in the South. It was usually cool and humid in this season, so G.g's headaches got better. He painted more and stopped carrying knives to the garden to kill trees. I bought him thick rolls of canvas, stretched on frames and placed them in the corner of the room. Both of us tried to avoid arguing over trivial matters, and took advantage of most of the time for work instead. The money I saved was enough to pay for a flight to the Central Coast during the year-end holiday. On a quiet remote island, we would hang ourselves in the air for hours with an exhilarating skydive, watch the deep blue sea splash white waves, zoom out into the overwhelming vastness, and let the wind sweep away all our gloomy thoughts. Then, we'd dive deep together to explore the reef, a magical feeling I'd never experienced.

Ever since the time I went to the fishing village with my student friend where I took spectacular bloodshot pictures of his accident, I've never really dived into the sea. For many years, while living in the city, I'd visit the ocean park to see the miniature coral reef model in the poor aquarium whenever I had the opportunity. Watching me move lazily between the chilly displays, G.g said I looked as lifeless as a mummy specimen controlled by a puppet string. I hid a wry smile, realising that all of us were turning into a school of fish locked in a huge glass cage, swimming lazily and lifelessly, eyes darting through the clear glass, disgruntled. And as the fish coldly returned their gazes to the human creatures, they pinned their motionless fins and opened their mouths to yawn. In the aquarium, we were as boring as the sea creatures: oxygen-deprived animals, mediocre specimens thrown out of the wild. So, I was excited at the prospect of being in the sea where the wind would fill our lungs with fresh, salty air. Similarly, G.g listened to me, trying to rekindle his habit of watching films.

G.g was topless, wearing only a pair of light cotton shorts with colourful patterns. His hands slipped between my thighs while his head rested on the small pillow. His legs were stretched out on the floor, surrounded by cans of juice and cakes. Towards the middle of the film, G.g began to lose concentration with a series of consecutive questions.

Our discussion went as such.

'Is he as ugly as the fat guy in this Capote film?'

'According to the documentary, he was different. It's not accurate to call him ugly; it must be said that he was strange and idiosyncratic, unlike this actor. He was elegantly dressed, but his height was modest. Many people have even considered him eccentric and cruel. No one understands why. Very few people close to him understand the murky void that lurks in that unpleasant exterior. The public behaves according to a default way of thinking, so they are the same; most of them are passionate about killing people, not bothered enough to understand the mental trauma of someone different. If they witness a stranger swinging a knife or pointing a gun at someone, people can only condemn in disgust. Behold, the killer! Get rid of him!

'Some people are equipped with a little knowledge, and whenever they smell money, they jump in to make a profit by analysing the causes of the crime. At first they sound reasonable, but they only, at best, touch the surface of the problem. As for the core, it is the most important and subtle thing—difficult for anyone to reach. This is partly because of fear of hard work, but also partly because it's like being an exploration drill; you must be firm and strong enough, but sensitive so as not to break or be knocked out. In order to fully understand a person's innermost nature, it's not necessary to rely solely on intellectual experience or scientific knowledge; it requires more coordination, a delicate blend of intuitive experience and the firm belief in the so-called human instinct—sometimes just the blink of an eye—to explain the injustice. That thread of understanding is fragile, but it's enough to connect two lost people. Though, in the end, one of them has to end his life. It sounds complicated, but it's really that simple.'

'Stop it! God, I'll go crazy. You're talking nonsense. It's giving me a headache. Please don't talk about your philosophies again, okay? It's too abstract for my shallow understanding. I just focus on the visual effects. In short, there he is, that fat Capote guy—isn't he attractive at all? Well, he belongs to the upper class, right?'

'Wrong! It was only at the time when the story took place, then that he was famous, that he became rich. He was a reporter at a major newspaper, wrote scripts for film studios, and worked with a group of A-class stars in the art world. Look at him—doesn't he look cool? I love the way he's holding his glass of wine and smoking a cigar. Arrogant, insolent, lonely and bored. To be honest, I like the pictures of his younger days better, especially the picture of him wearing a short-sleeved T-shirt with a sloppy collar that stretches over one shoulder, unremarkable. But the lines on that face show a different beauty, especially the eyes. His eyes are very special; a look that pierces the camera lens, as if they want to expose and swallow everything. But there is something bewildering and out of place in that look—they look terrible, like the eyes of a demon.'

'A demon tinged with sadness, burdened with worries and torments?'

'It's possible. But inferring about someone you only meet through films is inaccurate.'

'By the way, why does he talk so much?'

'He has a knack for eloquence. Listen, his voice is like the wind.'

'Toxic wind. Is he bloodthirsty?'

'I don't know. He really likes to drink red wine, as you can see from the film.'

'Has he ever thought of murder?'

'I don't know.'

'Then why is he interested in a murder?'

'He did it to write *In Cold Blood*.'

'Why did he want to write that book? Since the killer shares many moods with him, he sympathises with him too, doesn't he?'

'I don't know. It must have been a game of calculation, professional acumen, instinctive inspiration, or a moment of compassion for a heart that has suffered a lot. He wrote that we're not as different as we think. Maybe this thought brought him closer to the killer, anchoring his faith with the thought: I feel like we grew up in the same family, but Perry came out from the back alley and I used the front entrance.'

'Really? So what about us? Are we as different as we think? Did we grow up in the same family? If that's the case, then which one of us is the lucky one to come out from the front entrance? Or do we both secretly share that dark and narrow back alley, like Perry? And really, is the thought that haunts Capote, that he came out from the front alley, correct? Or was he mistaken perhaps? Does the light that society casts on Capote really reach the back alley where he belongs?'

'Don't put barbed wires into your words; don't make subjective speculations; don't spread doubt; and don't bring two different worlds together. In short, don't think too far ahead. Every alley is an alley, and whether before or after, we've walked through them a long time ago.'

'I can't believe I made it through. It seems that I'm still entangled in the back alley. Or who knows, worse, that I only stumble heavily on the doorstep? In many cases, the front entrance is fortunate to be bathed in a dazzling light that is just an artificial light source. Just as we are playing a game of drowning the sun, in reality we are trying to kill a reflection, an illusion. That light is inherently pathetic, crippled and artificial, isn't it?'

'Yes, maybe. But hey, we were so busy talking that we didn't pay attention to the film; maybe we missed some interesting details? Stop talking and focus on the film.'

'But I still don't get it. I'm curious—how many men has he slept with?'

'I don't know. But your way of thinking is implicitly offensive.'

'Who can control how the public thinks? Basically, he's talented and eccentric, isn't he?'

'Sure then.'

'But why do people make so many films about him?'

'Because he's eccentric and talented.'

'No. Because he will always be an abandoned, lost, lonely child.'

'We're like him. But we have no talent and we are completely anonymous.'

'But we have the right to step into the film industry.'

'Who wants to make a film about us?'

'We ourselves. We have some cameras, we'll shoot ourselves.'

'To make a film, we need to have a good reason.'

'Isn't inspiration a good reason?'

'But we're not Truman Capote.'

'Right. However, no one has forbidden us from doing so. We need to film ourselves. Because we're alone.'

'But we're together; how can we be called "alone"?'

'Wrong. Even if we have two or more of us, we are still one. We're unique. Don't try to project more than one self. It's just useless. If we don't preserve an image of ourselves, we are forever alone from birth to death without anyone knowing. Therefore, we absolutely need others to see that we once existed. Making our own films means a lot and it shouldn't be mocked.'

'Oh, have you already been influenced by Capote's eloquence? So where do we start?'

'From a conspiracy.'

'What conspiracy?'

'Let's carry out a real slaughter. On a real living body.'

'God! That's impossible.'

'Why not? Conspiracy to kill something really alive. The wolf, for example.'

'Don't do that. Don't break the oath. Did you forget? It must be a year before it's time to throw it in the oil pan.'

'Okay, do as you please. So ignore the wolf. What about the boy?'

'Which boy?'

'That neighbourhood demon that has eyes more dangerous than an owl. He always stands behind the rusty fence. He always spits out words inappropriate for his age. He thinks he's twenty years old or something. He drives me crazy.'

'What are we going to do with him?'

'One of us has to play the maniac killer. He will be the ideal victim for our first experimental film.'

‘The other person will take on the role of Truman Capote: note-taking, and investigation?’

‘Right. We’re going to record a bloody murder with some of those cameras. We need to practice making a film.’

‘Good. So let’s thank Truman Capote.’

‘Yeah. Thanks for inspiring us.’

‘Stop, we should go to bed. It’s two o’clock in the morning.’

‘So what? I like long nights. I hate it when the sun rises.’

‘We couldn’t kill the sun, could we?’

‘We failed to drown the sun in a pot of poison. We need to think of a more efficient way.’

‘Yeah, let’s see.’

43. a plea outside the gate

It’d been raining for many days. We stood on the balcony of the wooden house, eating a homemade cake. We were happy, at peace with ourselves, smiling silly. We ate and whistled.

The wolf hovered at his feet, patiently raising his muzzle waiting for the crumbs to fall. Suddenly the wolf snorted and barked towards the gate.

I turned to look and said, 'Look who's lurking outside the gate!'

'Oh my god, it's that demon-possessed boy', immediately the cake became stuck in H's mouth, as if he'd choked.

I was surprised at H's reaction and immediately asked, 'Do you know that kid? What's he doing in front of our house?'

'Let's go there and see!' H released the piece of cake. The wolf quickly grabbed it and ran away.

I hesitated, trying to look deep into H's eyes and asked, 'He's looking for you.'

'No. You should go out to see him. I'm scared. When I stood before him, I felt so stressed that it was almost like I were a mouse being thrown into a cat's cage. He used to say horrible things to me', H put a hand over his chest. I guessed his heart was about to burst.

'Okay, then you should go back inside. Remember, don't lie on the red sofa and complain of a headache. Let me talk to him. If he's insolent, I'll deal with him. Get your camera ready.'

H rushed inside the house, and I slowly went out to the

door. As I walked, I finished the cake. The scent lingered on my nose. I was craving more. I could even smell the rain from the surrounding leaves.

I didn't open the gate. Looking through the bars, it was clear that I was inside and the boy was outside, yet I felt like I was the jailer and he was the prisoner. But showing no fear, he latched his arms on to the rusty iron bars as if determined to open the gate. He didn't say hello, but kept his eyes wide open, half-wary, and half-threatening. I'd never be afraid of that childish look.

I raised my voice, 'What are you doing here? Are you stalking me?'

'I need to see the killer', the boy stated.

'You must be wrong. There's only me here. There's no bad guy like you say.'

'I saw him here. Maybe you've hidden him in the house. Let me see him.'

'Why?'

'I want to ask him something.'

'About what? You can tell me.'

'I can't tell you. Because you're just a shadow of the killer.'

I guessed there must've been something wrong with his mind. Perhaps he was delusional. Perhaps he was so into tragedies in the books he read that he took them as what happened in real life. His simile was idiosyncratic: 'you're just a shadow of the killer'. Fine then, I'd play around with him for a while, before turning the tide.

'You're wrong. It's me, it's me. Don't you recognise me, brat?'

'You? Don't think I'm childish. I'm twenty, or so.'

'Ha, ha. You're a liar, but you have a sense of humour. You're twenty? Look at you.' I watched him and couldn't help but laugh.

He didn't flinch or move; only his eyebrows were slightly wrinkled. He shouted, 'Shut up! It's just that I don't like growing up. But I've existed for twenty years. I have a strange disease that makes me stop aging forever at the age of ten. That's good too. Think of that as my camouflage.'

'Camouflage? Well, let's just think of you as some sea monster. So you meet the killer, ME, for what? Don't tell me you're looking for me to confide in.'

'I don't need to confide anything, to anyone. I came to learn.'

'What? What the hell would you learn from me?'

'Learn to kill.'

'You...' I gasped. My throat became constricted.

'Learn to kill, do you hear me?' he repeated, almost screaming. His voice was loud and resounding, like it was coming from a loudspeaker in an empty room.

I tried to control my stammer, 'But kill who?'

'My grandpa', he paused for a few seconds, to swallow and change his stance. He gauged the strength of the shock to see how it was seeping into my body, and then continued in a clear voice, simply and nonchalantly, 'Show me how to resolve conflicts. He keeps coughing. It was as if some feather was stuck in the back of his throat. He's tyrannical and demanding. He makes a noise that I can't stand. He can't walk either; he's glued to his chair and his eyes are glued to the television. Cough, watch TV and eat. Eat, watch TV and cough. He eats a lot of food. But he doesn't do anything. Worse, he's ready to hit me whenever he can, with a whip. He dominates my life. Why can't he and I settle the matter of life and death together? Life should go on for only one person: either me or him. One of us must die. The future belongs to me. He is useless and brutal. Doesn't he deserve to die?'

'That's horrible. Are you a human or a demon? It turns

out that you intend to do something terrible. You want to be free. You intend to destroy your grandfather as if you were slaughtering a chicken. Well, it's not that simple. Aren't you afraid of being punished by your parents?'

'My parents? Don't worry, they don't exist.'

'You're a liar. They must have run away from home, gone missing, died in an accident—or have you already killed them?'

'My mother died a long time ago. What about my father? Don't worry. If I meet him, I won't forgive him. I swear I've never met him.'

He and I both stopped to catch our breath. The surrounding climate was cool, but I felt that my body temperature had skyrocketed. I was about to burn bright like a flame.

Suddenly the boy fell to his knees, his eyelids lowered in earnest, his hands hanging helplessly, his voice whispering softly, 'Please, please. Please open the gate for me. Help me.'

My body temperature lowered but my mind was still spinning. Exhausted, I staggered away from the gate. I shouted, 'Go away! Damn you! You're evil.'

44. real conspiracy

Hiding behind the door, I could hear both of them. G.g's voice grew more shrill and panicky towards the end of their conversation, while the boy's voice was crisp, clear and decisive. That powerful voice knocked G.g down easily, just like me when I stood by the gate with the owl the other day.

It was strange—when G.g staggered into the house, the boy suddenly disappeared in a flash, even though I'd kept staring at the gate. I could see clearly that the boy was on his knees. Did he disappear into the rain? I was reminded of the time he melted against a sunlit wall in the same way. I didn't blink once but he disappeared. It was unbelievable.

G.g lay dozing on the red sofa with an ice-cold towel draped over his forehead. He had a fever. I brought a glass of water for G.g and waited for him to rest for a while. When G.g was really awake, I would work with him on our plan.

This time, I decided to make the boy disappear from real life. I would also smash the owl on the gate. I'd pierce the owl's eyes. The mindless bronze owl would turn into a zombie.

45. camera

He babbled non-stop. It was drizzling. The sky was murky. Occasionally he swung his arms and slashed into the air. He still didn't stop babbling.

46. p

'Kan, you must be tired today. Have you gone to bed early? I called but you turned off your phone. I wanted to tell you a story about a demonic boy who is my neighbour. I know you'll love to hear it. There're many strange things about this boy. Both times, I met him with the gates closed, where both of us were alternately inside and outside. It's like we were playing a game of imprisoning each other. It's late, but I wish you'd turned on your phone. I remember once you told me about your childhood—you also stood behind the gate waiting for your father. I want to know more about how you feel. What did you think then; what did you wish for, Kan? I'd like to ask you about some experiences you've had, so that I can make sense of that boy.'

He dropped his pen, his face fell on the table, but his eyes were dry. Who is Kan? I have never met this person. I also want to make a phone call, but I don't have a hand—I can't.

He pulled out the old postcard again. He looked at the picture. He lightly scratched the surface of the photo with his fingernails. He pierced the eyes with a knife. He cut off a head. He splashed red ink on the photo, smearing it. When he was done, he put stickers on the door of the storeroom.

Suddenly he got angry and crushed me. My body was covered with wounds. I was hurt.

47. p

'Mum, why did it rain that day? Why does it always rain when you're not here? Mum, I'm so cold. I don't have enough blankets. I'm hungry. He didn't let me eat. He also won't let me cry. It can rain whenever it wants. Why don't children have the right to cry, Mum? He slapped me. He pushed me outside in the rain, said, "Okay, stand here, you can cry as much as you want, when your tears dry up and the rain stops, I'll let you in."

Mum, why does he always yell at you, "Hey, bitch, is this bad boy my own son?"

Mum, why don't you answer? Your silence pierces my heart, deeper than a sharp knife.

Mum, it's raining again today. Every year it rains, I

cry less and less. I'm afraid that one day I won't be able to cry anymore, even though sometimes I know how to slap myself.'

He trampled on me again, this time with a blue highlighter. He makes me uncomfortable. I don't like shiny things. And yet I see he's got a bunch of colourful highlighters. He's too sassy. And who is his mother?

48. p

'Mum, there's food in the fridge, but I'm not hungry. Have you seen my dog?

God, he killed my dog! Mum, please stop him!

Why do all things I have leave me in the end, one way or another? When will it be your turn to leave me forever, Mum?'

49. p

'He pushed me out into the rain again. He dug a hole and said, "You come down here—lie down, I'll bury you like I did with your dog. Well, if you cry again, I'll bury you alive immediately, okay?"'

50. p

'Mum, I wish I could go back to the old days, where I was the one holding the shovel. I wish I was a hole-digger. I have a shovel in my house too, but it's rotten, it's melted into the ground. As soon as it was exposed to light it melted into the ground. Old things are rotten; isn't light capable of disintegrating them so well? Do I have regrets? I don't know. Anyway, physically, it no longer exists. Therefore, the small hole in the back garden can't be filled.

Mum, on rainy days like this, I feel so cold. I'm lying on the mattress wrapped in a blanket, but it's still cold. My back is like being soaked in ice. Am I still lying in that hole?

Get me out of that hole, Mum!'

51. p

Today, he didn't write anything on me anymore. Thank God, I was just exhausted.

Last night, one of us got caught in the fire. In the night, his eyes were like two deep pits, filled with red hot coals.

52. the first chance

I stood at the albino cemetery, looking at the bare ground and blackened rotten logs, surprised to find that the mushrooms were no longer growing. Were they too scared of my game? Poisonous mushrooms, where are you now? Poisonous things often had extraordinary strength and the ability to persist. So where were they? Or were they trying to trick me? Fine, I'll find something else to play around with.

I wish I could climb over the fence without a ladder. The other side must be another world. The world of the owl-eyed boy and his grandfather. It's been two days now, but he hasn't re-appeared. Many times I wandered in the garden, pruning branches to make noise, but no one appeared. Once, I tried to go to the neighbour's front door to peek inside; the house was silent, the door closed. I called but no one answered. How's the old man in there? Has the boy killed his grandfather? I didn't believe he could do that so quickly. He hasn't even set foot in my house to learn from me as he wished.

I couldn't wait forever, so I went to the storeroom to look for sticks to make a ladder myself. A bunch of broken slats tied together with old wires. The ladder was made clumsily, but enough to press on the wall. I stood on it for a moment, peering curiously over at my neighbours.

The house was still silent; the afternoon light landed

on the curtained window. The curtain swayed slightly as if the sunlight wanted to flip it open before it faded away. The mouldy corners of the walls were long and covered with vines. The house generally looked similar to mine, but gloomier. It was old, sloppy, very poorly lit. Surprisingly, in the garden there were so many suspicious little holes, with green grass, brown-black soil, swarms of termites and insects rising up. There was a pit of stagnant water; the surface was covered with dark scum. There was a solemn shovel-shaped hole, and tiny red wildflowers grow along the edge of the hole, looking like a blood rim.

I wanted to jump to the other side but the wall was too high. I had to take off the T-shirt I was wearing, reattach it to a strong rope, tie it to the top step as a fulcrum, whereupon I slid down the rope and dropped down.

As soon as my feet touched the ground, I suddenly heard a wolf barking in the alley leading to my house. Just then, the bell rang loudly. Who was looking for me? I was confused as to what to do. Hesitating for a moment, I decided to climb back up.

The shadow of a person loomed in front of the gate. There it was, that boy.

I crouched in the luxuriant tree. My heart wanted to jump out of my chest. Joy overflowed. God, I'd been looking for him for two days now. I made a plan. And now he had come to surrender.

H wasn't here. Without H, would I be able to trick the boy into the house and kill him smoothly? While I was killing the boy, who was going to film me? My phone was at home. I wanted to call H to come immediately. I would delay the situation by making some small talk with him, long enough for H to get here in time. Would the plan be exposed? Would I miss a precious opportunity? No, I had to come in; I needed to do this immediately, without delay and without panic.

The cub was still barking. I was getting impatient with every bark. My guts were spinning like a roller coaster.

The bell rang two more times and then went silent. I poked my head out of the leaves. The boy disappeared. I just sat on the ground and let out a long sigh.

I packed up the ladder and put it in the storeroom; I was sweaty and thirsty. I trudged along, unbuttoning the knots made from my torn T-shirt as I walked. The shirt H bought for me had only been worn a few times, not yet stained with any paint.

In the living room on the red sofa, the boy had been sitting there waiting for a while. His hands were leisurely folded along his thighs. He was looking up at me and smiling provocatively.

I was dumbfounded. My brain held one thought only—a single signal—that I was about to have a stroke.

53. p

'Date... month... year...

It was the first kill.

It turned out that killing someone was much simpler than we imagined. You could just take a glass of water to the victim and tell him to drink! Come on, drink it slowly, and then we'll talk. The dialogue would begin to flow, sometimes leaking, sometimes overflowing; we would turn our eyes to the corner of the room, where we hid a pestle, a long-handled wooden pestle with two big and round ends—quite heavy—an item that people often use at a restaurant to smash large blocks of ice in a sack, gradually breaking the ice into pieces. Why was that pestle in the wooden house? I really didn't know. When we moved in, it was already there. We didn't need that tool in the house, but it was there in the kitchen, looming, prominent, as if some all-powerful person knew our will, and he reached out his omnipotent hand to manipulate us. So, when I touched the wooden pestle, it moaned happily, as if it wanted to beg me to take it, as if it was telling me, "Don't think, don't hesitate—you only have this one chance: hit him! Come on, hurry up, or the boy will escape."

I grabbed the pestle. The boy didn't have time to react. His eyes were wide open, his hand holding a glass of water. He didn't seem to have time to understand what was going on, so I swung my pestle up and down with all my might.

I was beating non-stop.

As it turned out, hitting a human's head was easier than I thought.'

I was so disgusted that I almost fainted. He just slammed his fist on my body. Angry? Satisfied? I was headless, I wasn't a catfish. My body was flat. I was in pain. My enemy could only have been the fire. If he tore me to pieces, I would still be alive, though disabled. I knew his evil by heart. He would never tear me apart; when he was angry he often rolled me up and threw me on the floor. Then the wind would turn me over and push me around. The wolf would gently nudge and rub its muzzle against me. I'd bounce back as straight as ever. How many of my brothers had died from being set on fire. When we were alive, we were white, and when we died, we were black.

Oh, he hit me again. Was it disappointment or boredom this time? His eyes were wistful. And he continued.

'It turned out that it wasn't as difficult as I'd thought to bury a body. Fortunately, the boy's body was shrivelled, just a pile of shredded meat. He was so small and there was so little blood. The red colour hadn't spread throughout like I imagined. Without the overwhelming red, I felt terribly off.

While I struggled to turn on the camera, the wolf barked. Yes, bark all you want, baby! One day, not far from now, your fate will be the same as this kid. But it continued barking; the more it barked, the louder it got. Its snout was wide, its fangs white. I was angry. I strongly kicked him in the hip. It screamed and rolled out of frame. Damn it, I'd been filming for a few minutes already. That wolf messed up the filming; I'd punish it by starving it for two days.

Well, it turned out that filming wasn't fun anymore if you killed somebody that was so small. There was less of everything: less meat, less blood.

When I turned to the weapon, I was really depressed. I thought I was mistaken. Wouldn't a knife with a glint of steel make the footage livelier? But why didn't I think of using a knife at that time? Oh my gosh, I had a set of twelve knives of all sizes at home. I was so stupid. I'd ruined my own filming. Now I had to pay the price for this mediocre footage. Without H, the film wasn't shot in time, the footage was bland, and there was no sound at the climax. What was the point of banging the pestle forever?

Okay, this mistake, I'll fix it next time.'

Next time? Would there be a next time? He was crazy, no doubt.

I wish I could get on the phone to tell someone.

But I couldn't. He used a red marker to draw streaks on my body. Red splashing, spreading, overlapping, dense. I suffocated.

54. late nights

'The thing I asked you to do last time, how's it going, H?'

'What did you ask for?'

'Find a model. Otherwise, you have to get naked for me to draw.'

'Yeah, let me think.'

'You think for too long. I've lost all enthusiasm. I want it done this week. The holidays are coming up—I'm free for a few days and I want to draw a lot. Help me and hurry up.'

I suddenly thought of Kan. If only he would model for G.g.

I prepared a light dinner with a few leftovers in the fridge. Tuna salad served with boiled noodles, with cabbage soup and meat rolls. It took about ten minutes to cook. The canned tuna had been in the fridge for so long that it was only one month before its expiry date. I dumped the minced fish in the coleslaw, adding the cucumbers and thinly sliced tomatoes. Homemade medley—not too bad. Cabbage rolls with meat, ready-to-eat type in blister packs, presented with a few bulging, soft onion stalks. Packaged food! Packaged food! They also encapsulated my life, numbed my emotions. My whole body was like a portable refrigerator.

That thought made me terribly sad. As soon as I put the salad in my mouth, tears immediately flowed. I suspected it was probably because there was too much chilli. It's been so long since something got me to cry.

Suddenly I felt a strange pain in my arm. It was as if I had lifted a heavy load, or lifted something high and held it there for a long time. The pain was excruciating. I couldn't stand it anymore; I had to let go of my chopsticks and go to bed. On the bed sheet, there was a long, dry, dark stain in an arc, the remains of a strong splash of semen. Was it mine or Kan's?

When was the last time I slept with Kan?

Unlike G.g, who only liked doggy style, burying his face in his pillow, raising his butt, hunching his back for me to fill him from behind, Kan treated me equally in switching our roles. The posture that gave Kan the ultimate pleasure was the sixty-nine position. We would lie on opposite sides, clutching our thighs and buttocks, burrowing our heads into the most sensitive fork, then grabbing the iron ingot, holding it in our mouths, and then heating it up red. It got so hot that it melted; we merged into one, becoming a volcano on the verge of eruption. It was wild, heavenly pleasure.

Now, I reached over and traced Kan's back in my imagination, but only bumped into the expressionless, inflated pillow. I suddenly realised that this bed was too large; this room was too large, the dining table was too wide, the blanket was too large. Why did I suddenly realise that things in this house were too big? As wide as my heart right now. So wide that it became an abyss. Endlessly wide.

I grabbed my phone, took a deep breath, and called Kan.

55. the first murder case

It was raining. Why did it rain when I dragged the body

to the garden? After a series of rainy days and then a series of rainy nights, why was the rain determined to trap me?

I waited until it was late at night before bringing the body to the garden. I stuffed the boy into the sack, like I was dragging a large ice cube. Initially, I was going to put the wooden pestle in the sack. But I kept it in the kitchen, just in case. I didn't forget to clean the blood stains carefully. I even washed the pestle with lemon-scented soap, which helped to remove the smell of blood. If the blood was absorbed into the wood fibre, the blood would mix into the mouldy brown colour of the wood. I thoroughly erased the traces. I was sure no one would notice.

I did all this carefully, trying not to make any noise. I hoped that no one was stalking me.

While dragging the sack, I didn't hold the camera. I didn't think that this scene was attractive, not to mention that if you wanted to turn on the camera, you had to have the light on. I was afraid that the sight of me crouching and burying the sack would make anyone who happened to pass by become suspicious. They might call the police. No! No one should know about my crime. I had to erase the traces myself before dawn.

However, dragging the sack containing the corpse in the night wasn't as easy as I thought. I felt an invisible force clinging on to the heavy bag. My arms were flexed together, my legs ached, my body squirmed down and then bounced back. I was struggling with the sack.

Why was it so difficult to bury a child's body?

I finally made it to the albino tree cemetery. The ground was wet and muddy, soaked in rain. My shoes sank. I wondered where I should bury the body. The original plan was that when the burial was completed, I would erase the shoe prints, wash my shoes, and even plant grass to cover the ground. Without a shovel, I used a knife. I chose the biggest butcher knife out of the twelve, but in comparison, it was still too small, not as effective as a shovel. I dug into the ground, trying to focus on each knife stroke. It was hard work. Like a mouse. Like rodents. Like a burrowing cricket. It seemed that I was to dig forever.

The night covered me. It protected me, threatened me, swallowed me, and served as my accomplice.

While I was digging, something bristly, as soft as a feather, fell on my back, as gentle as a comforting hand. Through the raincoat, through the thin spandex I wore, it awakened all the senses. I almost shivered the moment that invisible hand slid across my back; it quickly sent a light, convulsive electric current through my body. I reached behind me, grabbed the feather and examined it. The night was dark; I couldn't see anything. But I assumed it was a flower. Why did the albino tree flower? When did it bloom, why didn't I know? I always remembered the outstanding feature of this plant was that it bloomed red flowers on rainy nights. But why?

I picked up the flower and put it in my pocket, then kept digging the hole. If only I had a shovel, the job would have been much quicker.

It was still raining. It was cold. The raincoat seemed to be punctured or torn. I felt numb because of the water dripping down my neck and shoulders.

I suddenly realised that it was easier to kill a human than to dispose the body.

56. room of the forgotten

'Every time we sleep together, it's always in the dark.'

'It's not planned; it's just a coincidence. We're all busy during the day.

'Besides, it's much more interesting to make love in the dark. Body defects are easily covered by darkness. We don't have to see any ugliness on display, so the euphoria doesn't die out prematurely. We're so enthusiastic about each other, not bothering to analyse anything; we're not ashamed at all. We're blindly bumping into each other, devouring each other crazily.'

'We are two fish that freely swim in the dark water.'

After the usual sequence of actions, wrestling, joking, provoking, teasing, rolling around in bed, licking, fucking, then exhaustion, we'd let go of each other, panting. We'd blabber on like that.

Kan got up and adjusted the light to make it brighter. He took out a towel to wipe the wet greasy drops on his stomach, and asked, 'By the way, are you free this weekend? Let's go to the fields north of the city to fish.'

I nodded, pleased. It'd been a long time since I went there to pick up water lilies and duckweeds with G.g. The thought that I was cheating on G.g made me miserable.

Kan walked towards the bathroom, his bare bottom quivering with the golden light, turning into a perfectly moving mass. Suddenly he came to an abrupt halt, as if he thought of something. Kan returned to the bed, looked at me intently, and asked, 'Why is the door to the other room closed? What do you have in there?'

I startled slightly, 'Which room are you talking about?'

'The attic. The room upstairs was very strange. You even stuck a picture on the door; it was slashed and cut, like an old photo of a family. Why is the man's head in the picture gouged out?'

'Oh, I see. It's the storeroom, where I keep the things I don't use anymore. It's so old and useless. I almost forgot about it.'

'A storeroom? It can't be useless then.'

'I keep things that I want to forget about in there.'

'Then why don't you just throw them all away? Or take out and bury the garbage in the garden? Wouldn't that be better? Why do you bother? I guess some rats have already set up their homes in there.'

'I tried to clean it up a few times, but I was afraid. I don't need that room anyway. Every time I think about opening that door, I feel nauseous. Those crippled things, the old memories that deserve to be buried behind a thick layer of dust, if I were to open them up, dig them up... I wouldn't be who I am today. I'd go crazy. So I comfort myself by thinking that it's an empty room.'

'How horrible. It sounds like a magic chamber. Does it contain your childhood? Or are you keeping a secret? Let me guess: maybe it's the room of sin. Let me try to open it. Well, a dried mummy would suddenly come falling forward; its white skull would fall to the floor, rolling around. Ah... Save me!'

Kan gave out a long cry after the joke, like an actor in a horror film as he ran around the room. We hugged each other, fell on the bed, laughing.

'It sounds interesting. Perhaps it should be that way.'

'If you're lazy, just say it', Kan said, wiping his tears from laughing hysterically. 'I hate ugly things in my house. So what I don't use anymore, I get rid of, including disgusting animals, like...'

Suddenly Kan paused, pondering for a moment, 'Hey, is the black wolf still alive?'

'You said you don't care about it anymore. Actually, I've already butchered it.'

Kan's cheerful face was suddenly covered with a layer of grey ash. He silently went straight to the bathroom, slammed the door, and said nothing. There was the sound of rushing hot water.

I thought I'd told a bad joke. I was afraid that because of this, with his temper, Kan might refuse to model for G.g. If so, it seemed that I would have failed to keep my promise with G.g, and then our relationship could become strained.

57. trust

'How dare you do that in my absence, huh?' H's voice

slammed into the air with angry whips. He threw the camera on the bed, his face red.

'Look, we still have many more opportunities. It's been two days since that kid has disappeared. But his grandfather never left the house to look. No one has suspected anything. The proof is that if he had been reported missing to the police, the police would have already been hanging around here. We're so lucky. Don't you see that?'

H was still angry. He grabbed a beer bottle from the fridge, gulped it down, and walked around in circles. I was so scared of this kind of circular movement; it looked like he was possessed by a demon. I waited to see if he unbuttoned his shirt, and climbed on the roof again. He perched on the roof, like a bat, or an insect perhaps. Could I then shove him into the air and help him fly like in Magritte's painting?

After draining two cans of beer, H began to press his face close to mine, drawling, 'You're a selfish, evil bastard. Come up with a new trick to make it up to me right away, get it?'

I flicked the finger that H was pointing at my forehead, saying, 'Right now? There's another person waiting for us to kill him.'

'The boy's grandfather?' H's eyes were bright.

'This time you will take action. And I'll be holding the camera, okay?'

We put our heads together, the laughter burning our brains.

58. first drawing session

H brought a guy to my front door and winked as if to say, 'Here he is! Talk, and do whatever you like,' and disappeared.

I rubbed my eyes a few times. I couldn't quite believe that the guy in front of me wasn't a mannequin. Such a perfect body? I wanted to touch him, trace every line and rip his clothes off at once. But I didn't dare to do that. I held back, boiling off the worst of my thoughts to ease the throbbing tension between my thighs, and quickly, I shoved rudeness into the depths of my crotch, hoping they wouldn't rise uncontrollably again. Brutal attempts of the will to suppress instincts often fail miserably; I knew it too well.

He was right in front of me. There was a reserved smile on his lips, foreign, as if it wasn't his own.

Next was a series of forced movements of strong arms,

deep but interrupted breathing.

I wanted to take that breath away and collect it in a glass jar, and then pour it all over the back of my neck.

We shook hands.

I led him into the room and brought him water to drink. He smiled at me. The new smile was really for me.

He asked permission to go around to see the house; he touched everything, then he said this house was so strange. He didn't use the word beautiful. It seemed that 'beautiful' didn't exist in his vocabulary. He went upstairs.

It was my drawing room. He looked it over and took it in entirely. He nodded, saying he liked this and that. He was like a curious child exploring every nook and cranny. But there was still one place he wasn't allowed to set foot in: the storeroom, the dirty, disorganised, slightly rotten, rusty room.

I knew what was in there: the pestle that I used to hit the boy. I moved it from the kitchen to that storeroom.

He frowned slightly and immediately returned to his normal expression. He asked for permission to take a shower.

He locked himself in the bathroom for a long time. I imagined him enjoying looking at himself in the mirror, looking at his body, and scrubbing. He must've been the type of person who loved himself too much. I guessed that he must've been cold and selfish.

Outside, I prepared a seat for him. I carried the red sofa into the drawing room and then set up the easel and painting tools.

He stepped out with a towel wrapped around his body, his wet hair hugging his face. His skull was round, well-proportioned. The square chin loomed over the shaved beard. He looked around, guessing where he would sit and what he would do next. The shawl that was loosely wrapped around his body hung over a small diagonal stripe, dangling at his waist, like the shape of a peculiar cell.

He was reluctant at first, 'I accidentally wet all of my hair, is it okay?'

I said okay, and pressed him to the sofa. I posed for him. I wanted to rub against the chest that was breathing heavily. I instructed him to sit in a sullen posture, arms crossed over his head with the look of hidden suffering.

I put a cup of water on the chair next to me, reassured him that when he felt thirsty, he could just signal, I would bring him water. 'You have to try to keep your posture, focus, not move. While I'm working, you shouldn't say anything.' I told him. 'Okay, can I take the towel off you now?' I asked. He nodded, looking at me intently. He was prepared when he did this. It was thanks to H's advice and detailed explanation. I was grateful to him.

I stopped breathing for several seconds when I could clearly see a naked body up close. He looked confused for a moment, and then quickly focused on his work, keeping his mouth shut. The hairs on his thighs and belly were still dripping with water.

I was terribly thirsty, but still held the pencil to the canvas.

Kan—H's colleague—was he really the one who gave me the wolf? He didn't look evil. Or did I just drink a cup of enchanted water?

59. camera

They became one on the red sofa. The two men were making love on the red sofa. Their bodies were red, like two boiled shrimp.

The two shrimp were flexing, stretching, spreading, bouncing, banging their heads, probing their antennae, kicking their tongues, squeezing their limbs, arching their spines, rolling their eyes back, biting their lips, closing their eyes tightly, opening their mouths, biting the air, panting, stretching, snapping feet into the air, slithering gently, squirming, squeezing, screaming, groaning, stooping, shivering, falling apart, their heads bowed, haggard, stretched, drowsy; they were panting wearily, and then they passed out.

For the first time, this happened in broad daylight, in the wooden house.

There was a lot of milky liquid on the sofa, which quickly turned into stains, and were difficult to clean.

Outside, the evening came. A dog howled vaguely into a dull space.

60. camera

'Go away! Creepy creatures,' a man shouted, his mouth twisted, his pupils wide open, furious.

A blurry, scratched film.

That voice repeated, 'Go away! Creepy creatures. Go away! Creepy creatures...'

Gothic music emerged, evoking medieval melancholy, pushing back the mutated image into an unknown realm.

61. massage game

H pulled out a clay pot and placed it at the foot of the bed, saying, 'These feet work hard all their lives, but we rarely know how to take care of them properly. Let's soak them in here. They need to be treated well.'

It was a big, deep pot, filled with hot steaming water.

I put my feet into that pot, feeling hundreds of tiny needles gently touching me; they smoothly transmitted thousands of tiny heat currents, making the soles of my feet tingle, but it was strangely refreshing. Thin waves of steam wrapped around the calves, caressing the feet. I closed my eyes, enjoying each stream of sensations crawling down my spine, rushing to the top of my head, spreading to every strand of hair. Every centimetre of my skin was raised; I had goose bumps all over my body. I couldn't close my mouth anymore, but had to let out a long, secret groan; the sound of my indulgence lingered. It was soaked with wet steam, lazing right in front of my nose.

H's voice rang in my ear, 'See? Dip your feet in the water. Go on. Don't open your eyes.'

I followed his words, my eyes still closed. When the soles of my feet touched the hot water, I couldn't hold back the loud moans of pleasure. I knew I'd be exploring a magical foreign land, as if my feet were set on clouds.

Right! Clouds! Feeling light, I was about to fly up from that cloud.

'Go again, deeper.' H whispered to my ears, his tone of encouragement was gentle, mixed with exhilaration. I put half my foot to test the heat, and then, feeling safe, I began to dive deeper into the water. H lightly waved his hand so that the sprays of water spread evenly all over my legs. Hot water dripped in a stream from my thighs to the calves; I shivered irresistibly. My breathing followed the flow of the water, mixing with the sound of water lapping under my feet. The pot suddenly turned into a boiling sea, immense and endlessly deep. The toes waved on the water surface, no longer bending and stretching, the water currents rubbing and caressing. Then they touched something long and slick, wobbling and twisting in the water.

'What are they?' I asked, startled.

H laughed softly, 'Just a bunch of medicinal herbs I picked in the garden.'

'Really?' I rest assured, not bothering to open my eyes. In many cases, the world seen with closed eyes would expand infinitely, capable of morphing into a million things. The leaves were cooked in a pot, like soft seaweeds that followed the movement of the feet, with a strange scent. Medicinal herbs? I didn't even know that there were medicinal herbs in the garden. Oh, this scent was like a mixture of lemongrass, basil, mint, and something more than that.

As if he could read my mind, H suggested, 'More than that. An unexpected, odd mix. By the way, please don't open your eyes.'

'I give up. I can't guess. My imagination is limited. I lack clarity on everything. I'm not Magritte who could picture the surreal world. I don't know how to name abstract smells. Tell me, what is it? Is it the smell of crushed albino leaves? Or their floral scent? The only flower that fell in the night, I hid it in my pocket; it was already disintegrating and no longer had a specific shape. I can't imagine what they look like when they bloom. Why do they only bloom late at night so stealthily, like a criminal? That dangerous tree is terrifying.'

The water was still dripping, like so many small streams spreading from the thighs to the calves, merging into the deep sea. Each splash of warm liquid was spreading continuously, echoing a crackling sound.

H's voice mixed with the running water. 'Guess again. Do you feel comfortable? Or should I say euphoria? Soaking our feet like this in a hot tub: it's such an easy treatment with the leaves I pick in the garden. It's such a simple thing, but why haven't either of us ever thought of it? Free the feet, release the feeling. What do you see, G.g?

Do you feel like your feet don't belong to you now? It's as if in the blink of an eye, some hand snaps them out of our hip joints, and swaps someone else's legs into our bodies. They are strange, but lovely. They are not legs, they are sensual entities. Isn't that right, G.g?'

'Yeah, almost', I swallowed slowly and let out my moans. 'I think I'm happy. I've almost fallen in love with these new legs. H, you really know how to make more creative games than me. Right, because you're smarter than me. You always help me think of more unique games. Oh, I feel like I'm about to fly. I will fly, like in Magritte's paintings. By the way, H, tell me, I beg you; this strange scent is smothering my nose, paralysing my sanity, and is drowning me in this delirium. What exactly is it?'

The roaring sea below suddenly stopped moving. There was silence. Our breathing seemed to have stopped altogether. Through inertia, my feet still slid under the smooth earthenware basin. A pair of fingers gripped a few elongated, sticky leaves. Big toe curled.

'Say it. Say it, H', I smelled the unusual smell.

'Do you really want to know? Okay—so open your eyes. The foot massage here has ended. That's the smell of blood.'

I was startled awake. I opened my eyes. It was a basin of red liquid.

62. inspiration

It wasn't my fault, nor was it a joke. It wasn't the only thing I killed that day.

Did a viper bleed that much? Did its blood smell so bad? That unfortunate snake; I honestly didn't want to kill it. It was just because I couldn't distinguish a viper from a vine. It was a mistake. That was all.

The neighbour's goose—what did it do? As soon as it saw me, it quacked loudly, non-stop. I hated it because it loved to do a dog's job. I didn't want anyone in that strange house to hear its unusual alarm. So I first lured it to charge at me. I waited for it to stretch its long, aggressive, confident neck, and when it opened its beak wide and snapped at my feet, and I immediately grabbed its neck, clamped it, and twisted it, hard, decisively. Its neck was broken; blood gushed out. It was simple. It was forced to die for daring to threaten to spoil my plot.

Killing a goose to get closer to one's goal wasn't sinful.

But its blood was terrible; it seemed to flow forever. Would a goose spew more blood than a boy? To the point of infinity. So why couldn't I mix them with the leaves to make a foot bath?

Snake blood and goose blood were mixed together, giving off a fishy smell. How should I take care of it?

I carefully erased this fishy smell by mixing the blood with half a tablespoon of five spices, and some tea leaves. I even squeezed a few drops of fresh lemon into a basin of water. But it wasn't perfect, and in the end, the smell of snake blood and goose blood couldn't be erased. It shot up G.g.'s nose. He had a very sensitive nose.

I didn't expect G.g's mood swings to be so bad. He killed quite a few things before, but I could never anticipate how he would feel afterwards. He pulled back from the leaves, mouth agape, almost shouting. His knees were raised high, almost touching his chin. Half of his leg from the calf down was dyed red, and his toes were soaked in drops of thin blood. Then, after a moment of terror, the gaping o-shaped mouth suddenly stretched into a smile. He laughed, giving way to a sudden, violent outburst of joy. And he slammed his feet into the earthenware basin. Blood red flakes splattered out.

The water became cold. I sweated profusely.

G.g grabbed my shoulders and shook me, still with that ecstatic face, his voice muttering, 'I know what I have to do. Blood. I need to extract that old man's blood, soak it in this basin, and steam my feet. Hot water, hot blood. That old man. Right! Another opportunity will come, this time more useful than the last. You have inspired me. Thank you so much.' G.g poured a rain of crazy kisses on my face. Then, still holding my face in the palms of his hands, he asserted with a gasp, 'You must work with me this time. With you, the filming would be perfect. Come on, let's begin the second killing!'

63. the second kill

We made a noose, mixed in a variety of colours, a composite of moss green parachute cords, peeled electric wires with iridescent red copper threads, gaudy tinsel, and finally, we stuck countless pieces of barbed wire into it. At first glance, the string looked harmless and clumsy, like a child's homemade toy. But the noose was strong with its hidden thorns, seductive and sparkling.

'This is perfect.' We looked at each other, half-smiling, and nodding in satisfaction, and then we covered our heads with black hoods, leaving only the eye sockets. I thought this image was as cheap as it was an extract from a film, but it was the optimal choice.

We carried the ladder out of the storeroom, against the wall. We treaded lightly on the neighbour's lawn. No goose was around to stand guard, because it was killed yesterday. The space was quiet, surrounded by tense breaths.

One of us walked along the wall, towards the main door. The other crouched down to the ground, closed the back door, slipped his hand into the crack, and opened it. The old man would probably notice a knock on the door. If he was in a wheelchair, he would have a harder time. Perhaps he would scream for the boy, but of course, there would be no response. As the man timidly put his hand on the doorknob, about to open it, he focused on the stranger floating in front of him, when suddenly, a few strides away, another stranger would attack him from behind. The noose tightened. The old man yelped and waved his arms and legs, unable to understand what was going on. Meanwhile, with a series of precise and flexible movements, the killer's hand calmly strangled the old man's neck, wrapping a few more loops of rope. First, the rough layer of the glitter wire would touch the neck, rubbing it hard, causing uncomfortable itching. Then came the soft layer of the parachute cord that approached, tightened, nullifying the itch. Next were tiny red copper threads with deadly power and the effect of sharp blades, slicing flesh. And finally, the piece of barbed wire would pierce the old man's throat, ending the excruciating pain. He was breathing hard, struggling, trying to untie the noose desperately. It was too late. The next loops of wire wrapped around the old man's arm, sealing off the resounding breath that had just died. Soon the old man turned into a blunt mass, a bound, restrained object, stuck to a chair, unable to move.

Thanks to the rope, that tethered object knew how to shine and sparkle.

We turned on the camera and started recording from the direction of the door. The frame was full of light. The camera moved to the side of the subject, dropping down from the top of the head, rotating around the body. It was a skilful, perfect shot. The tethered object was illuminated and studied carefully under every angle. The object had stopped breathing and stiffened from time to time.

Finally, we removed the object from the chair and laid it down on the floor. We prepared a bucket of water mixed with blood: red, viscous, concentrated. The bucket of red water was soaked with many rotting leaves with only the tendons left, like a school of strange fish swimming in a basin of blood.

We then poured a large amount of blood on the object lying on the floor. Schools of bony fish were released from the cramped prison pond, joyfully pouring down like a waterfall.

We adjusted the light and the camera angle, making sure to film up close and in the distance, to capture everything we did. The object was crushed, finely chopped, bruised, and tattered.

It was a frenzy.

64. camera

They were rocking the wooden attic, playing around with a bunch of dolls.

65. p

'Date... month... year...

We completed the second kill.

Wore out. Detached.

To avoid trouble and prevent any slip-ups as we transported the body, I decided to bury the old man's minced flesh and bones in his own garden. Carefully and skilfully, I cut the layers of soil that had smooth grass, planting over the hole I dug. I'm sure that after a while, everything would dissolve into the ground, leaving no trace. As for the skull that couldn't be broken, I brought it back and buried it in the albino cemetery. Even if it became a zombie, it would be a zombie isolated between consciousness and form. It would be busy searching for its own integrity, without enough power to ravage anyone. Even if the police were to investigate, they wouldn't be able to find it. I was sure it would be very difficult to discover any clues. In addition, the time to track down its whereabouts and connect the evidence would certainly be enough for me to escape.

I hope that something like that would never happen. Now, I must rest assured and indulge in the pleasure on the tip of my tongue. Anyway, my friend and I succeeded perfectly in the second killing.

I sigh with relief.'

66. the third kill

The next target was the owl.

Smashing the copper owl wasn't as easy as we thought. It was horribly solid. We took turns spinning the hammer to hit its head. The hammer recoiled and I almost hit myself. Our hands were sore, bruised and swollen.

We smashed harder, even wearing thick wool gloves to avoid friction with the handle, but it still didn't work. The owl wasn't harmed, only slightly dented; the paint was only scratched a little. The most terrifying were the owl's eyes, which kept swirling on each hammer swing, as if taunting us, 'Look! What can you do to me, huh?' Half teasingly, half contemptuously, 'See? You guys failed. Do you want to do something more? That's it; you'll never amount to anything!'

In the end, we succumbed to exhaustion.

I didn't think it was a mere copper owl. It was the

embodiment of evil.

We panted, mulling over it. Finally, we took it to the garden, dug a grave in the albino cemetery, and buried it alive.

I still wasn't sure. The plan was that in the future, if I found out about some copper foundry, I would bring the owl there to melt it. I wanted to destroy its haughty image, especially those piercing eyes. I grew ecstatic when I imagined how the fire would encircle and blind its eyes, melting it, destroying it.

Before that day came, however, I might have to endure the threat of its phantom rising from the moist soil. I had to try living with that feeling.

67. p

'Date... month... year...

We failed in the third kill.

I'm uncomfortable. But I believe that one day, not too far away, I will take care of it satisfactorily.

I'm just procrastinating.'

68. p

'I know, just a few more days until Sunday. Kan will come for his appointment. I will continue to draw a new picture. I'll make him do a new pose; it'll be hard to see. I want to study weird poses. I hope he agrees.

I didn't expect him to look so pleasant. He was more excited than I expected. He didn't even accept payment even though I mentioned it many times. I like fairness. I hired him as a model, he should be well paid. But he refused to take the money. He said, "I don't need money. I'm doing this for fun, because I feel like I mean something. You even gave me more than a sense of pleasure. So don't ever mention money again if you don't want me to stop doing this. This isn't a game; I'm serious."

I listened to him. I'm really happy. I'm satisfied with him.

But why does he sleep with me so willingly? Does he do the same with H? How many times have they made love?'

69. p

'Mum, why was I sent to school to learn how to observe the world, how to analyse thoughts and how to think, without ever learning how to defend, fight and control the bad things that come from inside me? I was taught that humans are a

first-rate species, endowed with superior features, but not how humans can be barbaric. I was taught that the universe is infinitely vast, but I see that the human heart is deeper than that universe.

Mom, why didn't anyone teach me from a young age that sometimes, we need to kill something to find our inner peace?

I practiced killing quite a few things before proceeding to the human body. The first time, I was shaken. However, by the second time, I'd mastered it. I've known how to execute all actions so that they are neatest and most effective as desired. I have definitely cleared up a family, including an old man and his grandson. Both, in my opinion, deserved to die. For what? For a reason that only I know for sure.

There is only one thing that greatly disappoints me. Killing a living thing, regardless of species, is really not difficult. But to kill a deeper form, their dark spectre, which hangs around and is present all the time around us, is not easy.

Mum, tell me, should I kill them after all? Will I be able to do that? Is it so present that we need to destroy it? Or are they too elusive, like the illusion when I drown the sun? Maybe I'm intoxicated with constantly killing a shadow, eliminating an illusion without understanding the essence of the problem. I've done this twice, on two bodies, and plan to continue—but what do I get? Don't let anyone tell me it's a crime, or something like a guilt complex. It isn't! I'm not that stupid.'

70. p

'Mum, did you ever know who I was? Have you ever imagined what it would be like when two men sleep together? You could never think of that, that's for sure.

The mind is always hindered by consciousness. And we are so different from each other. The gap between us is so vast. It's the same as the time when you were standing by a river while I went swimming in the water. I was suddenly swept away by a current, but when I called for help, you couldn't save me because you never learned to swim. Even when it happened, you couldn't even grab a lifebuoy, a wooden plank, a banana raft, or anything that could float, to throw it down for me to cling to. You didn't have those things around you. Mum, you gave up on me.

We were both helpless, so we pushed each other further apart. For what reason? Not a torrential current, of course. But because neither of us were prepared to respond. When we looked at each other helplessly, it was as if we belonged to two different worlds. Understanding couldn't come just by looking, even if it was a look of empathy.

So, if you saw me having sex with a man, I'm sure you'd be shocked too and wouldn't know what to do. I couldn't even think about what would happen if I saw myself. Perhaps you'd think you were hallucinating.

Hallucinations: we often attribute what we can't understand to hallucinations, and yet we can't help but still torment ourselves.

We witness the plight of others but we have our own problems, and we struggle to find solutions to no avail.

You are on the riverbank and I'm always in the water; it will always be like this. So we look at each other as if the other were a hallucination.

Mum, don't ask me why I love killing and making love with men. Before that, I conducted an experiment on a chair. I crippled it, and then I imprisoned puddles, tortured mushrooms and the trees; I cut off objects, twisted the neck of a goose, and smashed many other things. Because I found pleasure in doing so, as if it was my endless source of joy. After doing such horrible things, I'm often inspired to start a new painting. I know I'm creating beauty based on destruction.

You may ask me why I choose this barbaric method. Why? Because this is the meaning of my life. I care only about my own feelings.

There are hundreds of other ways out there, but why do I find meaning in destruction? Mum, don't ask such stupid questions. In my case, I believe it is necessary and right. I must kill all the things that need to be killed in order for my life to be peaceful.

Sometimes I wonder, if I kill them, will I be okay? Or if I fail, will I survive? Anyway, to me, killing is almost a religion.

Mum, I'm tired now, I need to go to sleep. It looks like it's going to rain. It's cold on rainy nights like this. Mum, the July rain is always colder than other times of the year, isn't it?

What do you usually do on rainy days in July, Mum?'

71. different face, different eyes

Around three o'clock in the afternoon, my comrade called and told me to find a way to leave work and come to a film première. It was the film by the fat, short, brash and paranoid director we met when he introduced the project to the public.

I couldn't even remember the name of the film, and most of the film's content. At best, I could remember some of the actors' names.

We yawned and our eyes teared up. We took turns asking when it would end; we were only interested in guessing where the main actress had done her plastic surgery. We giggled after each sentence as we analysed the mechanics behind her beauty; we discovered a lot of weird things. For example, the cute and compact shape of the nose was definitely Korean technology, but the bridge of the nose was too high and straight, looking too artificial. As for the size of the breasts, they were a mixed product, and besides, some of the semi-nude scenes in the film didn't provide enough data for us to infer the typical procedures for fake breasts.

She waved her hand, trying to look thoughtful, 'I can't stand it. Even as a woman, I'm inexperienced in guessing the origin of fake breasts. I don't even know how to explain what artificial fat, salt bags or silicone are. It's another territory. Sometimes I feel embarrassed because I have these modest breasts—I don't look sexy, do I? Men rarely stare at me. It turns out that was the cause. But regardless, I'd rather accept this than having plastic surgery. I'm afraid of pain. Besides, I can't stand the thought that the fluttering thing on my chest is actually a bag filled with something.'

At the end of our sincere and ironic conversation, we clasped our heads together and laughed so madly that our hands clenched tightly against the arm of the chair. Our whole bodies shook like we were having a seizure. Of course, no one dared to laugh out loud.

Anyway, it was the weirdest comedy I'd ever seen. After leaving the screening room for about ten minutes, I laughed when my comrade whispered that I actually forgot to zip my pants when I got out of the toilet. This time, it was her turn to confuse the name of the movie, but she clearly remembered the name of the leading actress, the one who had undergone so many plastic surgery procedures.

We strolled down the noisy street. The sun was burning hot. I thought we were two pieces of fresh meat rolling around on the grill, about to burn.

Suddenly I blurted out, 'Have you seen any films by Truman Capote?'

She shook her head and looked into the distance. 'But I know who he was.' Then, all of a sudden, her eyes brightened, turning incredulous, 'What's up?'

I looked deep into her eyes, hesitated for a few seconds, and timidly whispered, 'You look like Harper Lee. No, I mean, I think what you are to me is almost like what she was to him.'

We came to a sudden halt, almost colliding into a few people behind us. She froze, opened her eyes wide, motionless, hung a sharp gaze in mid-air, then suddenly stuck the metaphysical needle into my pupil, causing me to rub my eyes with pain, so I had to look down slightly. Thin dust curled under the heels of our shoes; they moved wildly in the monstrous afternoon sun. Something terrible was going on in that look.

Her lips moved, 'Which means...' she hung in there, and then turned away quickly. We walked side by side, not saying anything.

'Almost. That's the situation I am in. Sorry!' I broke the silence.

Involuntarily, she smiled, mumbled, 'Capote and Harper Lee, I understand what you're talking about', and disappeared around the corner.

After that, we avoided each other for a long enough time. Perhaps she was uncomfortable, and that inadvertently formed a gap between us. Understanding or disappointment? I'd never thought she'd be insensitive, but it was probably because the story unfolded so suddenly.

72. G. world

Kan texted me during work. 'How about we go out tonight?' 'Where?' 'Secret.' 'Cool?' 'Surprise guaranteed.' 'OK.'

At six o'clock, Kan and I left the office, and turned in two different directions. Soon we were mixed with the rushing crowd. At work, no one ever found out that we'd been seeing each other for a long time. Both of us knew how to hide and we were good at camouflaging. We pretended not to show any intimacy, even maintaining the same tone of speech as before.

Twenty minutes later, we met at another location.

I followed Kan into the large, solemn, multi-storey building. People dressed politely came and went every now and then. The ground floor was used as a place to sell stationery and it was quite empty. The floor plan was hung on the wall along the ground floor walkway, showing that from the first floor up, there were four to five real estate offices, two law consulting offices, and an acupuncture therapy centre. Other than that, there was nothing else written. It looked sketchy. I couldn't believe a building this big had only so few offices. I didn't know what the remaining floors were for. That was a secret.

Kan pressed the elevator button; we soared to the thirteenth floor, the last floor.

The elevator was running smoothly, indicating that this building was quite empty, or we were lucky at the right time. The door to the room opened, and Kan stepped out into the hallway, straight to the room at the end of the hall, very confidently as if he had been familiar with this place for a long time. I followed silently with my hands in my pockets, my heart pounding, biting my lip as I swallowed the excitement in my heart. I felt like I was walking into a secret room, about to meet some leader of a secret society.

Ignoring the small bronze sign engraved with the words 'Traditional Therapy Centre', Kan approached the closed door that also had a bronze sign on it, on which was engraved 'G. world'.

Kan gave me a signal, and we both pushed open the door and slipped in. The door wasn't locked.

Again we walked through a long, narrow corridor. There were recessed blue lights on the ceiling. Two muscular young men stood by as security guards, wearing tight pants and open-breasted shirts, each with clean faces. They coldly extended their hands to direct us inside.

The end of the corridor opened to another world: hot and strange, the real world of G. world.

There was loud music. Warm, yellow lights lit the room. Behind the thin red curtains, a huge lake was evaporating. In that lake, a group of men in semi-naked sculptural poses stood half-submerged in the water, holding a fake bronze tray carved with delicate patterns, the tray surface lined with glittering printed cards that looked like bank cards. On the lakeside, visitors came from all walks of life, standing and sitting in various postures, playing and joking around. There was no sight of any woman.

Kan looked around for a bit, then bent down to pull out two cards from the tray. He dragged me into the adjoining room that was fitted with clear glass. Kan handed over his card at the long computer desk and paid a large sum of money to the male employee in office attire. He received two other slips with red stamps and scribbled letters, and walked out again.

We walked to the other door, showed those two cards to the two topless security guards in shorts, and received a friendly smile and pat on the shoulder.

Inside was our world of complete freedom.

Kan said, 'From now on, do whatever you want', and jerked his chin, ordering me to take off my clothes. Kan did it first, quickly slipping off the layers of fabric, including his underwear, and then stowed it all in one drawer of the stand, lined with dangling keys. Then, Kan pulled the towel hanging loosely over his shoulder.

I followed him; my mind was as black as if it was dipped in ink. The core inside me had left. It wandered off somewhere, giving up the empty shell that was my body, and in the next moment, another me was about to come in. That other me would walk, talk and do what I really couldn't predict. I was wobbling in shock, because everything had happened so suddenly. I was overcome by an uncontrollable surge of excitement after a series of images I had just seen with my own eyes. Leaving my mind blankly glued to the world around me, I frantically unbuttoned the last button on my body, following Kan's example.

I staggered after him, like a naïve schoolboy who put all his trust in his teacher. We waded into the oval lake, which looked like a giant bathtub. Countless ceiling lights were delicately arranged, shining just enough light into each small tub, emitting a blue halo (Blue again. Why not yellow or red? The owner of G. world must have been obsessed with blue. Or did he have a reason for designing the lighting in this way?). In each of those little water boxes, men's bodies lined up with their arms and legs stretched out, their eyes closed, sinking into their own realm. From above, they looked like mummies well preserved in formaldehyde solution. It was a quiet and dark space. There was a soft sound of water splashing, which was immediately swallowed up by the classical music leaking from the small speakers on the wall. It sounded like falling rain.

The whole public bath scene was like an exhibition installation, where the silent dolls were submerged in water and light. No one would know what happened when one of the nude dolls suddenly jumped up.

Kan and I quickly became part of those mummies in formaldehyde. We lay next to each other. The water was warm. Only then did I smell the sweet scent emanating from the surface of the water. Kan whispered, 'Just clean your body, soon someone will come to take care of you, to help you relax.' I could immediately guess what he really wanted to say.

Sure enough, a moment later, a man in his thirties, wearing a swimsuit, walked over to the tub next to him, bent over, put his hand on Kan's chest, and gestured, 'OK?' Kan smiled, half-closed his eyes, 'Outside, just a little bit', then nodded at me, 'I have a friend today. We will do it together. Give me some privacy.'

The man nodded and walked over to the shelf where there were bottles of all kinds: body lotions, shower gels, shampoos, soaps, and mineral salts. There were also cotton towels and all kinds of back scrubbing and massage tools. Then he walked over to me and Kan, dangling his legs in the water, perched on the bulkhead, motioning for the two of us to turn around. Then he started rubbing our backs with a sponge soaked in milk. He controlled his hand to turn from one person's back to the other's back, sequentially, rubbing evenly. The movements were mature, sometimes fast, sometimes slow, sometimes strong and sometimes light, sometimes sliding along the spine, sometimes around the waist, sometimes deep into the hollow of the buttocks, sometimes gently squeezing the nape of my neck. I shivered constantly. I'd never experienced this feeling. No one had ever done this for me. He rubbed and massaged my bare back with a bath sponge. I felt like all my worries were melting away. My whole body flexed and rose to the rhythm of the hand movements. Now I understood what it really felt like to be taken care of. No, not the feeling, but the enjoyment of the pleasure. Such a simple thing could give immense pleasure; why hadn't G.g and I done it for each other before?

Beside me, Kan started purring. The man paused for a moment, as if measuring the effect he had achieved, and then continued to splash water on Kan's bare back; the foamy soap ran slowly down into the lake. Kan let out a hiccup, crouched down. I looked like I was hypnotised. The man poured some more shower gel onto the cotton pad and turned to me. This time, the smooth strip was out of rhythm; it started to accelerate and move wildly, I couldn't tell how every inch of my skin would react to this. I felt goose bumps all over me. I closed my eyes tightly, biting my lip so that my moans wouldn't break the general silence. Suddenly, the skilful massager's slick fingers slipped into the deepest part of my buttocks, poking around there for a while, making my entire lower body squirm. I still dared not open my eyes, partly out of embarrassment, partly out of fear of Kan. Kan must have seen my naughty movements. On the other side, Kan's breathing was interrupted as if he was trying to control himself. And then I couldn't take it anymore; I came right under the water. A sob burst out in my throat. I clutched one hand to the side of the tub, while the other hand slipped beneath me to keep the manly thing in my palm.

The man continued to rub my back again, patted me a few times as encouragement and comfort, then pressed two fingers firmly on the cervical vertebrae into a finishing blow. He finished, stood up and stepped on the shore. Water gushed from his thighs, washing away all the tiny white foam clinging to the hairs of his legs.

Kan rolled his eyes at me. His expression looked eerie; he drilled a point into my flesh, stinging. I averted my gaze from Kan. I dunked my body to the bottom of the tub, as if only the overwhelming blue water could shield me from that gaze, and in an instant the desire to die in the pool rose inside me.

73. the lake in the sky

I staggered down the deep corridor. The same topless guards with symmetrical faces and sharp square jaws like carved stone, cold and beautiful, were still standing there. They opened the door and held out their hands to see us off. Everything that existed on this high floor felt unreal. Even the gentle scent from the swimming pool lingered in the cold air in the hallway. It clung to me, seducing me, as if every scent molecule had already clung to the layers of my clothes—or maybe they had already taken root in my skin.

I didn't know what time it was. This time, the order changed. Kan walked behind me. Since leaving the public bath, we hadn't said a word to each other; my mind was occupied by the blue light, which spread in front of me under the floor; I wobbled like a drunkard. Yes, G. world got me drunk. It knocked me off my feet with that magical blue lake. I had a feeling that I would come back here again and again, with or without Kan.

I pressed the elevator button and waited. I still endured Kan's piercing gaze. We continued to remain silent. There was something more unusual about him than me. How could I know what he was thinking? No, I'd never be able to do so.

When the elevator door opened, a stranger stepped out. He was forty-five years old or so, with many folds in his face. He had a high, broad forehead, and his hair was slicked back with gel. With this hairdo, he looked like an intellectual by the way he dressed. He looked over my shoulder, focused on Kan, and said in a low voice, 'Hi! We haven't seen each other for a long time. How are you, Kan? Is this your new friend?'

Kan awkwardly mumbled something. They shook

hands. The stranger reached out and pinched Kan's chin, as if he were petting a child, a gesture that showed that they had known each other for a long time. Giving an inexplicable smile, he turned to stare at me from head to toe. He unconsciously pursed his lips tightly, tensed; his nostrils fluttered like an animal sniffing, then he walked away without saying a word. He strode gracefully toward where we'd come from, his butt bouncing up and down.

I could see that his eyes were filled with melancholy. I guessed the people who came here often had two types of eyes: one was sad and empty, while the other was excited and happy. There were probably only two common states. Regardless of the extremes, the purpose of coming here was still entertainment and forgetting the world for a moment. Would G. world help them get rid of all their sadness? Did they get any joy out of leaving? Or would they be loaded with new concerns like me?

We drove out of the parking and stood idly by the side of the road waiting for each other. I wanted to say something to Kan, but I couldn't speak. Had someone locked my mouth shut?

While waiting, I looked up at the sky and the crescent moon. From where I stood, the moon was entangled behind the building, casting a weak halo around the messy architectural lines. The sky glowed artificially, like a giant piece of leather stretched between two blocks of streets. Suddenly, I saw a dark lake appear in the air. It slowly floated across the narrow night sky. There was a familiar figure crouching in the lake, like the carcass of a skinned frog soaked in formaldehyde. Bizarrely, it was G.g. I saw him rise to his feet, diving violently into the lake. He swam frantically, and it was clear that he was completely exhausted and disoriented. Without a doubt, G.g was drowning in that deep puddle, trying to send out a desperate cry for help. But did he actually call out?

Just then, from behind, Kan let out a warm breath on the nape of my neck, whispering in my ear, interrupting the silence, 'I'll follow you home, okay? Right now', and gently patted my shoulder.

I blinked, startled. The lake in the sky had disappeared.

74. whip

'Whip me! Whip me again! Whip me more. Wow... Don't stop. There! Hands up. Ouch! Faster. Again! Whip me again. Whoa... Whoa...

'The medieval music became more ferocious and melancholic. It soon filled the room. They were locked up, layers of sound stacked on top of each other, twisted, unable to find a gap to escape.

'The man groaned at length. The string of pent-up syllables popped out of his throat, contorted, while his body writhed in bed. He was on his knees, crawling and sprawling out like a tortured snake. Of course, he wasn't wearing anything.

'Kneeling, arms bent forwards at the elbows, he tilted his head upwards at an angle of about fifteen degrees. His thighs were wide apart. With that posture and his white, naked body, he looked like a frog with its skin peeled, patiently waiting for its prey.

'The bait was the lashing of the whip.

'The frog's face deformed with each convulsion. Its mouth opened wide; its tongue was filled with foam, it groaned incessantly, and it soon reached the climax of its orgasm, sending a strong stream of semen onto the bed.

'The whip wove on that white body with red, intricate motifs. After a while, they turned purple.

'Occasionally, the frog even burst into tears, but tried not to. However, the puddles of water on the sides of its nose and wet eyelashes betrayed that secret. The wrinkles on the face folded up, hidden and lonely.

'The first time, I was so surprised; I asked why. He didn't answer; he said that it couldn't be explained. The main cause may have been an unconscious mania, manifesting uncontrollably when he fell into a state of being in a powerful trance. Specifically, from the whip.

'I said, "You're a masochist, aren't you?" He remained silent. But I stopped asking more.

'I hugged him. My trembling hands traced each pattern I had woven. I also realised that my heart was being whipped many times by a metaphysical force. I wanted to burst into tears. But my tears wouldn't flow.

'We kept hugging each other, kneeling on the bed. Before my eyes, the space of the room was distorted and discoloured. The table lamp was dripping with blood-red light, and the walls were stained with blood.

'From then on, I became his lover, and for a long time, it was synonymous with a relationship with pain mixed with pleasure.

'But I'm not a sadist, so every time I had sex and tortured my partner who was ten years older than me, my heart was filled with pain. I used to like tenderness, so every time I saw his bruised back writhing under the whip, I couldn't stand it and gently held back. But he wasn't satisfied and cried out in supplication. "Stronger and faster, baby!" he said. Many times I tried to give up. He said it was his own orgasm, and that I should just make him happy for a moment. And I did everything he said, I tried to satisfy him, to do everything for him, but not for me. My emotions had been completely dipped in a pan of boiling oil since the first time I swung the whip.

'Anyway, I still loved him. Honestly. He loved me very much. He knew how to make gentle caresses whenever I asked for them. He bought me many gifts, guided me to read good books, listen to good music and watch meaningful films. Although he worked as an engineer, his aesthetic sense wasn't bad at all. When he was a child, he was given music lessons, so he basically knew how to play a little bit of classical guitar. I asked him why he didn't try to cure his masochism. He laughed, saying there was no cure, unless he could overdose on something to finish off his life, and that was it. Then he told me not to worry about it. As long as I was there, he'd be happy. He revealed that his previous lovers also quickly left him, because they couldn't stand the gruesome scene in bed; some even vomited while doing it. Red blood scared them, he said, and forced a bitter smile. He loved me very much, a kind of grateful love. I dreaded that gratitude.

'Then I left him too, ending a relationship that lasted about two and a half years. Two and a half years of living in seclusion in a red veil of deformity. I was depressed and emotionally exhausted. I dismissed the idea that there was something morbid in our relationship. The whip was just a tool aimed at sensuality, a sex toy on par with other sex toys. Brutal, but a form of richness, perhaps. But I couldn't banish the pain and sorrow; on the contrary, I realised that it burdened me more and more heavily every day. It made me miserable every time I was with him that I almost broke down. After all, I still couldn't stand the whipping, which was synonymous with violence. I personally carried out that violent act. I loved his bruised body, I loved my hands, and I loathed myself.

'A crime perhaps?

'Sometimes I wonder why I think about him so much. Was that really love? To this day, the question is still unanswered. What dense fog has enveloped my brain, making me feel nostalgic when my consciousness had stagnated? Before him, I had never been with anyone for a long time. But I had to leave him, leaving behind a frenzy of whips to satisfy him, to the point where he and I were both exhausted. Was it a crime to end everything?

'After that, I read scientific documents about masochism, and I understood many things. There were experiences far greater than what scientific knowledge could describe, things that sink deep into our subconscious, things that we have to live with for the rest of our lives, things that often call us up at the moment. In the middle of the night, it hangs me from the beam, suffocates my heart, pours poison into my mouth, cuts open my stomach with a sharp knife, puts barbed wire into my crotch, and awakens something in my heart. It was more than a crushing, overwhelming humiliation, much greater than physical pain or emotional loss. It was an impotence of feeling. The feeling of being at the bottom of an empty hole, pushing us into a fog with no way out. A feeling of hopelessness that makes me want to die.

'Sometimes I thought if I were him, how would I live? Or if I had sadism, would I have made love to him by tormenting him enough to kill him? God, every time I thought about it, I went crazy.

'Why am I telling you this? You know, because it has something to do with the man you saw in the hallway leading into G. world. The one who shook my hand. That was him.

'And for many years after that, I couldn't properly fall in love with anyone. Every time I was about to have sex with someone, they would take off their clothes, and I would see their belt. My consciousness was still engulfed in that thick fog at that time, so I wasn't be sure if the belts existed in reality or not, but I swear I always saw them. Yes, leather belts. They lay shackled on the waistband of their trousers, squirming at one end with a metal corner flashing menacingly, like the head and tongue of a disgusting venomous snake. It turned my memory upside down, forcing me to return to the whip of that day. Everything showed up clearly, so many details unfolded in layers; it was clear and vivid, including the bloody red walls. I'd be shocked and lose all interest. Despite trying all sorts of ways to stimulate my penis, it would not become erect. My partners would be bitterly disappointed; they'd feel humiliated, and they would curse me in rage, thinking that I'd cheated on them. I was helpless. To make it worse, some of them, unable to contain their anger, even spat at me with a great deal of contempt.

'As a result, I was stressed for a long time and did not dare to get close to anyone. Being alone, unfortunately, inflated the empty balloon inside me, to the point that I almost exploded. Later, I found myself losing contact with reality, almost like there was no gravity. I walked on the ground as if I was flying. I longed for something to keep me grounded, because hovering in the air all day long made me dizzy, anxious and terribly confused. I became more irritable, ready to quarrel with anyone under any circumstances. It was an attempt to puncture the small hole that could help the balloon to deflate.

'Then I met you—no, I found you, because we've worked together for a long enough time, so I decided to try it with you. Yes, I hang out with you just because I've never seen you use leather belts, or even if you do, perhaps the fog that covered my brain has already disappeared.

'Please confirm that in the time I have known you, you have never worn a belt, have you?

'Yeah, that's it. Now I'm reassured. You see, I have never used them either. I don't want to see any more of those whips.'

***

Kan seemed exhausted after telling his story, a story full of strange things. Taking a sip of the warm water that I brought him, he let out a long sigh as if trying to release all of his fatigue, and then he slowly fell asleep. I looked at Kan's body, motionless as a corpse. I saw disordered patterns appear on Kan's wide back. I gently traced it with my hand, silently counting the red whips in my imagination.

Oh whips, please don't lash out at my memory. I really want to say goodbye to you.

75. camera

He said, 'There is nothing remarkable about this garden. Just a small hole where leaves fall and form thick cushions. Lie down there and listen to the buzzing of insects, the sound of dry leaves rotting in the sunlight through the canopy... All your troubles will disappear.'

76. camera

He said, 'There isn't much in this room. Only a bathtub for one person. Lie down, close your eyes, listen to the sound of water dripping from the shower, and you will see all your old memories as they rise and flow down the drain.'

77. camera

He said, 'There is nothing great in this man. Just an abyss in his heart. Don't get into it, no fire can warm the void, no breath can fill it. Let's dig, every corner leads to the vast...'

78. suddenly, a hole

Lately, I've gotten into the habit of lying in the bathtub for a long time. The water was warm enough. I even hung many pictures all over the wall. There was a long wall depicting the blue sky, white clouds floating in clusters. Entering the bathroom, it felt like I was flying in the sky.

For a few days, when I was bored, I erased everything: the blue skies, the blurry white clouds. They all went down the drain hole. I replaced the scene with bright red flowers and tried to recall whether it actually matched the shape of the albino flower, hoping to stretch some of the spiritual inspiration that had been lacking. Then I came up with an unexpected visual effect: as I lay deep under the tub, opening my eyes, I saw the flowers bloom painfully like blood spots. I splashed water on a flower; thin layers of wings flowed out into a stream, and finally, obediently went down the drain hole. It was exciting.

I planned to redo many more drawings. Perhaps in the near future there would be puffer fish. Those thorny balls, I imagined, might not look nice at all, because they were toxic. I was always excited about things that were toxic.

Dissatisfied with the background, I started to install the lighting. I added dangling lampshades designed in a natural way, shaped like honeycomb or anthills. There was something lurking in the landscape, like the gaping palate of an aquatic species stalking its prey. I enjoyed the work and I was sure H would appreciate it. He was just like me.

The toilet was large, so I had much freedom on how to decorate it. I thought the interior of a toilet should be very lively and different, so that every time I entered, I would feel as if my life had changed, lost in a new scene. After coming out, maybe I would have changed into a new, more attractive person.

I thought it must be significant in one's life to have one's inspiration in tandem with hallucinations.

After much planning, I decided to add a phone that

would hang on the wall above the bathtub, which would allow me to reach out to someone at any time. But hardly anyone called, except for a few familiar work-related calls. Of course, my conversations with H often took place in bed, not in the bathtub.

In the tub, my attention was directed to the window, a small parallelogram thing with slightly warped, misshapen edges. Over time, the glass became stained and opaque, changing colours depending on the weather outside. This window would suddenly become a TV screen.

Through that TV screen, I knew it was autumn, but some rain still fell, like a lost child of the weather who had arrived late. The wind blew strongly, a bitter cold. The albino tree shed layers of dry, curved scales, its branches swinging like threatening arms.

One night, I heard the wolf barking outside the gate, an unusual, stammering bark as if the bad man had stuffed a piece of poisoned meat in its mouth. Or perhaps it was frightened by the threat of some terrible force.

Right after that, the phone rang. I picked up the phone. On the other side, H's hoarse voice filled with fear, 'G.g., be careful. There are some strange people hanging around the gate outside. I guess they're the undercover cops; they're sniffing for the trail. Are you sure the corpses were destroyed a long time ago?'

I crawled out of the tub. The phone fell to the floor, sank to the bottom of the tub and wobbled, pushing the shivering air bubbles up to the surface. My fingers trembled almost uncontrollably. I dipped my hand in hot water. It didn't help. Did I really kill those two people?

I tried to stay calm, pulling the towel around me. Why was every muscle still twitching like this? I looked down at the tub, it wasn't a tub anymore; it had turned into a black hole, a deep black hole that emitted red vapour.

79. what if I was captured

So what?

Interrogation. Or torture. Imprisonment. Judgement. Torture (or interrogation). Imprisonment. Judgement. Brought to a scaffold, and bang!

If I had better luck, I'd be on trial.

A life sentence.

I'd die still in prison.

I'd be a zombie in prison.

Permanent imprisonment.

So, for example, if you get caught, it's best to get shot.

If I don't get shot? It'd be a life sentence.

Then no one would visit me. I couldn't even hire a lawyer. No one would dare to make excuses for me.

Conclusion: if, for instance, I got caught, I'd need to find some way to end my own life. It's the optimal plan; the only one.

80. what if I ran away

Don't try to escape.

I'd never be at peace. Danger lurks in all corners. I'd have to think about escaping all the time; I'd have to live in fear, stress, and insecurity.

I would never be free. I would never truly live. I'd just merely exist.

Even if life is short, it is only a temporary situation. I'd get caught in the end.

What if I got caught?

It is a vicious cycle. Everything leads to death.

81. other scenarios

There were no other scenarios.

There would always be that vicious cycle.

Capital punishment or suicide? Come on, you must choose!

82. of course, go to H

H couldn't save the situation. We were both depressed and confused.

Well, it seemed that my fate was decided. No, *our* fate: that of the two accomplices.

What kind of gun would they shoot us with? One shot, or more? One or more pellets, the result would still be death in the end. Plus, would they shoot us in the head or in the chest? To the forehead or the heart? Or both?

Terrible. Horrible.

Why weren't we terrified when we killed the other two? That was the difference between killing and being killed. But we won't get killed, since that would mean the blame would fall on them. To be precise, they would stuff our heads with the phrase: proper punishment.

No, it was impossible. But what should we do?

Actually, H wasn't as smart as I thought. In other words, his intelligence was limited. What an absolute disappointment. But that didn't mean despair. At the end of the day, there was still a tiny glimmer of hope to cling to.

My hope in H had faded, but its seeds could be planted in someone else. I needed to find a person to cling to. Yeah, who would that be...?

83. who knows, in the hole

I kept thinking about how to erase the crime. My mind was tortured to the point of explosion.

Explode! Explode!

I took a shower. I didn't know what to do but take a shower. I locked myself in the bathroom.

I buried my body in the bathtub. My thoughts wanted to burst out in my head.

Luckily, I didn't die in the bathtub. All night long, my body was soaked in the bath and became swollen; my skin was pale, the fingernails and toenails were bruised; the soles of the feet were pinched, like the leaves of a frozen lettuce in the refrigerator.

The moment I got out of the bath with a swollen, exhausted body, hope suddenly sprouted in me.

Hope wasn't sown in others; it grew in the folds of the

brain itself.

Here's the hope: find a way, by all means, to eliminate all the sniffers out there. That was the only way I could eliminate the danger.

That meant there were other scenarios.

That was to say, those undercover cops would have to meet their fates, but it wasn't clear how yet. But this garden was still large enough to accommodate many corpses, many more corpses.

So in the hole... who knows?

84. next plan

The morning was dry. The sun hid in the clouds at the end of the horizon. We hid under blankets, burying ideals in illusory dreams, hoping to prolong the illusion for longer, before we were humbly shaken into reality once again. We then threw our dreams into the gas stove, set them on fire, then grumbled into the toilet, then staggered out, opened the refrigerator, choosing a mood mask that had been preserved throughout overnight in the freezer, put it on, and went out to the street.

The street was deserted. It was Sunday.

On Sundays, animals ran wild. We ran round and round without knowing where to stop. We couldn't think of any viable ideas to kill the people lurking in front of the house.

Of course, we didn't see their faces. But we knew for sure they were there. We always felt that way. At night, they wandered around like ghosts. They perched on the roof, clawed at the eaves, as silent as an owl stalking a mouse. At night, they leapt over the iron gate, landing gently and quietly without making any noise, like a wild cat in pursuit. At night, they slithered over fences, swinging from tree branches, squeezing through window openings, undulating and dangerous, like venomous snakes taking their prey. They could fly like predatory bats, swarms of black shadows darting through the trees.

We didn't want to fall prey to that. In order to escape from our unlucky fate, we kept running on the road.

We ended up exhausted. But we still couldn't think of a solid plan.

We were distraught.

85. glue the cloud to the night sky

When I returned home, it was dusk. The beautifully

shaped clouds began to disintegrate, giving way to a long grey cloud that suddenly appeared midway. Its sharp curves were like a rudimentary mud-stained wheel that crushed the beautiful blue sky. On the horizon, another darker cloud swarmed that crude wheel, dyeing everything in black. The wind raged. A waterfall poured down from the sky, so fast that it was impossible to turn back.

Anyway, I got home.

G.g was dangling from the rafters like a bat—no, like a cloth puppet. The puppet stuck out its red tongue. It was terrifying.

'What are you doing?' I shouted.

'Practising', G.g. still hovering in the air, his arms outstretched, looking at me teasingly. Above his head, dozens of dark clouds hung low. They jammed up together, sealing the ceiling.

A cloud hovered and wobbled for a few seconds and then fell heavily on my head. I grabbed it, crushed it. The cloud fell.

G.g smiled, 'You look like a wolf in water.'

'It's raining heavily outside. The wind is fierce.'

'I don't care about the wind and rain. This place is absolutely safe. With training like this, it won't be long before I can fly.'

'Come on, come down G.g. You're boring me. Fly, fly, fly—why are you always thinking about that? Flying isn't as good as we thought it would be. It's like floating and wobbling. I know a friend. He's terrified of that floating feeling; when it inflates like a balloon, he just wants it to deflate so that he can be on the ground again. There is nothing better than equilibrium. It makes us feel safe. But you like to fly—that's a dangerous game.'

'A game? No, it's my desire. Remember, Magritte's *Golconda*, the flying people, remember?'

'No! They're just a bunch of idiots. Watch out, you'll turn into one of those idiots. Come on, please come down, G.g!'

'What did you bring for me?'

'An escape plan. We have to dig up the bodies and check if everything has really decomposed. If we can prove an alibi, they will definitely leave us alone.'

'The corpses? You believe they're still there after all these days? Skin, flesh, bones, hair, teeth, all crushed, dissolved into the ground, turned into green grass. Even if we try to look for them, we won't be able to find them.'

'But what about the skull—the old man's skull?

Remember, we couldn't shred it. And the black owl too. It's the evidence against us. They are in the business of uncovering this case.'

86. camera

He babbled non-stop, laughing and crying. He did all sorts of weird things in the storeroom. He used multiple cameras at once to record his actions. He didn't stop killing.

87. p

'I went to buy a new shovel. I searched around in the albino cemetery. I worked so hard to dig up the grave, but I couldn't find anything. The black owl had disappeared. Who had the upper hand? In the end, I decided to dig up every nook and cranny in the garden. I'm so scared. Could it be that they were one step ahead of me?'

88. p

'I can't do anything. I can't eat anything all day. I starve the wolf. It barks all the time. There's no one outside the gate, isn't there? Starving, it lies mourning on the steps.'

89. p

'I wanted to get out of this situation, but not knowing what else to do, I called Kan. Perhaps painting something would help me temporarily forget reality. Fortunately, Kan agreed.

After each time I dug, I drew.

The process repeated itself. Kan showered, modelled, and we made love after finishing the painting session. When Kan left, I started digging again. All over the garden, everywhere was ploughed. Holes appeared all over the garden, the green grass was ploughed and ragged.

Occasionally, the order was a little different; making love, painting, showering, but in the end, I still dug. I was tired.

I lived like that for a week. The number of paintings piled up. Sadly, no one watched. H did not come, using excuses to avoid me. Why did he run away alone? How dare he leave me alone to deal with fate? Did he betray me?

Now I only have Kan and the wolf.'

90. the hole no. 1

After many days of hard digging, the result was a small trench running along the wall. In the dark evening shade of the tree canopy, I sat on my knees, resting my hands on the handle of the shovel, wiping away the profuse sweat that had covered my body. Silence enveloped the space of solitude.

The wolf approached me, biting the hem of my jeans lightly, and looked up at me with wet brown eyes. Its tail was drooping by its side. I knew it was hungry.

I didn't know when Kan left. Now it was just me and the wolf. I thought I had to make dinner for both of us. We trudged wearily into the house.

I ate a ham sandwich, gnawed on the shrivelled lettuce leaves left in the vegetable drawer, and then took some leftovers from breakfast—pasta mixed with canned fish—and poured them into a bowl for the wolf. It chewed lazily.

When I finished, I quietly retreated to the bathroom, filling the tub with warm water. I lay down in my hole again, solemn and familiar, like a ritual. I closed my eyes. Every speck of blood bloomed painfully in my mind. The water was warm, but my heart was cold. Not a single phone call rang. I fell asleep in my hole.

91. the hole no. 2

He ordered, 'Where did you bury it? Dig it up now!'

Rain started to fall. It was getting dark. He clutched the bottle of liquor under his arm and repeated, 'Where did you bury it, huh? Dig it up for me now!' I cried out, looking for excuses. 'Dad, it's cold, I can't. Let's go tomorrow, Dad.' 'I said right now. Hurry up!' He swung the bottle close to my face, 'If you don't pull the body out, I'll bury you alive. Understand?' 'No', I resisted weakly, receiving a smart slap. 'I will bury you alive. How dare you steal my meal, you brat.' His voice rose like a wild animal. He chased me out into the garden.

I walked out into the garden in the pouring rain, without a hat or a raincoat, drenched and shivering like a cornered rat. He walked right behind me, asking, 'Where is it? Oh, how dare you disguise it with this lawn, you little brat. Are you trying to deceive me? Come on, hurry up, get the body out.'

With no other choice, I had to dig. First the head appeared, and then its front legs. I hugged my dog's body. He grabbed the hind legs, turned the dog's body upside down and dropped it on his lap. He laughed triumphantly. 'You tricked me, you dared to steal my meal, my drink.' He kicked me in the back, knocking me to the ground next to the hole.

My dog, my friend, had died the day before because of a poisoning. I buried it, but he forced me to dig it up and give it to him. He started a fire and burned the dog's body to have with his liquor.

I crouched on the steps, hiding behind the door, watching the little dog's body getting toasted by the minute. The dog was only a year old. It didn't die in peace. Why was my father so evil? It was impossible to stop him.

While sipping his liquor, he spotted me standing behind the door, glaring at him with hateful eyes. He angrily grabbed me by the neck, threw me into the yard, and shouted, 'Do you feel sorry for it, huh? Is this dog your son? You want to take its place?'

Then I found myself half-buried in the dog's hole. He went back to drinking, tearing the little dog apart. It died a second time: dying without peace. As for me, I've died a thousand times, so I didn't feel anything. I could only grieve for my poor dog.

The rain was still falling and it was getting dark. I fell asleep in the pit.

92. sling no. 1

'What are you doing with the bathroom?' Kan asked. After the drawing session was over, we were lying on the floor munching on juicy green apples.

'I'm decorating the wall so that it won't look monotonous. I've also changed the colour. What do you think?'

'It looks kind of terrible. The red looks scary. I've only been in there for five minutes and I can't stand it—it's hard to breathe in there. It feels like I'll suffocate to death.'

'If you don't like it, I'll erase it every Saturday. When you come here on Sunday, everything will be back to normal.'

'Ah, no, I'm just honestly describing how I feel; I'm not asking for anything. You seem to be getting more and more bizarre. What's going on? You can tell me, maybe I can help.'

'Um... I'm not sure what the hell is growing inside of me right now, or what I want in particular. But I always remember what happened...'

'Do you mean your past? Tell me: is it as horrible as the stories I've told you? I know how I struggled to get out of it.'

'I know you're better than me. I'm still in the process of resisting its control. Each of us faces different complex problems.'

'Maybe so. And why do I never hear you talk about your

family? The picture that's on the closed door of the room upstairs, the one cut out with holes in it... is it a photo of your loved one?'

'You're only half right. Those are my loved ones, but I'm not sure if they love me, or if I really love them. I've asked myself many times but never arrived at an answer. It's as if I were a small fish thrown into a puddle of murky water, struggling every day with a meagre amount of oxygen, thrashing around in those cramped conditions. Then, when I was about to lose hope, I was rescued by a sudden rainstorm, allowing me to escape from that puddle. In the end, my life was saved and sustained by such a well-timed chance; but this meant that my efforts to thrash about in the mud were futile. Since then, I have had the harsh habit of always breathing hard. My life is a series of constantly laboured breaths.'

'What put you in that state?'

'One of my loved ones.'

'That person is...'

'My father.'

'What did he do to you?'

'He abused me.'

'Oh... Go on.'

'You can imagine a man who chooses violence as his raison d'être. From the time I became aware of the world around me, I also learned to keep things hidden deep inside me. But memory sometimes insists on its return. Layers of memories crammed in storage compartments would suddenly leak out, forming a large, dirty, smelly puddle. Like a magic mirror that shows one everything, it would cruelly force me to go back in time, to re-witness the noisy fights between my father and my family members. Over and over. Alcohol and fighting. He even did it to my mother in front of my siblings and me. He pushed my mother on her back in the middle of the house, or rode on her back, torturing her. It was cruel, insolent and disgusting. While my brothers and sisters cried and ran to a neighbour's house to take refuge, I could only stand and watch. So he grabbed me. He threatened me, growling, "I'll gouge your eyes out if you keep looking. Close your eyes, now!" My eyes were still wide open, my facial muscles were stiff. He then poked his finger in my eyes, shouting, "Aren't you listening? I'll gouge your eyes out!" I ran away, not shedding a tear. He continued to beat me. He said he would beat me until I knew how to cry. Of course I won. And as a result, I became a target for all the beatings. I did it for my siblings. While he was hitting me, I thought, I really don't know how to cry.

'It went on like that. I still couldn't close my eyes and

ran away when I saw him beat my mother. I couldn't count the number of times there was hair grabbing, making love and tormenting. At that time, I wished I could go blind. And I poked my own eye with my finger. Only then did the tears flow. Later, I realised that I could never cry when someone hurt me; I only cried when I hurt myself.

'Violence, I think, must have brought him pleasure. The constant abuse eventually pushed my mother out of the house. And she left me. It was a dire situation; the bitterness suffocated her. She didn't have enough time to gather it all up, that's for sure. She couldn't take me with her, maybe because she was already too tired. My brother and sister fortunately took on the roles that had so burdened my mother. She had too much to bear. And so she had to leave me.'

'Did she ever come back again to pick you up?'

'No! Never. Maybe she was too scared. Not hearing from her made me think, maybe those three people died in a tragic accident. I couldn't hold a glimmer of hope. To be honest with you, sometimes a faint glimmer of hope also makes people miserable because you keep waiting. But if you put everything in the category of "dead", or "disappeared", then you can be freed from that anxiety.

'Since the day I lost my mother, I feel like I've been uprooted. Like plankton, I drift through vastly different regions without wanting to anchor my life to any specific thing. I become a stranger everywhere; I don't love anyone, nor have I believed in anything. I've turned into an extreme religion in which I've also become a believer.

'I often claim to be a flying tree. Yes, I can fly because I have no roots. I feed myself with empty indifference, plus a little hidden pride—the feeling of being able to live without having to find your roots or love anyone. I don't have to suffer any pain in this condition. It's something I'm most satisfied with.

'However, I attained this state only later in my adult years, when I had come to terms with the concepts of "dead" and "disappeared" in relation to my mother and my entire family. In fact, the moment my mother disappeared, I suddenly turned into a punching bag for my father. He beat me furiously. He packed all his hatred into his punches; they were stuffed with the helplessness that stemmed from the stealthy departure of his wife and children. A king who was shunned by all his subjects; the removal of a tyrant's power. He was left alone in his own game of thrones. He was fighting against the feeling of defeat, one that a circus owner or a puppeteer might have. The animals had escaped. The puppets had already broken their own strings. He stood alone with the rope dangling heavily in his hands. He had become useless. Something had to be done to make the hands less redundant. So he knotted the nooses, squeezed my limbs and twisted my neck. He dragged me away, as if pulling an inert stone, a rabid dog or a stubborn cow. He turned me into an exhausted vehicle, with which he went towards his goal.

'He practiced boxing.

'However, the sandbag was light, and the boxer's ambition to win was big, so he could never be satisfied. The more he punched, the more frustrated he became. Instead of reaching for a heavier sandbag to match the advanced exercise, he angrily pierced the sandbag with an iron awl. The sand melted away, leaving the empty shell. It's bittersweet—a useless empty bag with holes in it, like wounds that won't heal.

'I'm that empty shell: cold and indifferent. After so many long years.

'My love is a tiny pile of sand inside, but it has fallen through the holes. Sometimes, I try to fill myself with so many other things, so many unnamed memories. As a result, the bag either swells, being as light as cotton wool, or it shrivels like a carelessly stuffed haystack. It lingers in me, so meaningless and so flammable.

'Do you think it's sad?'

'Too bad. Hearing your story makes me feel I was more fortunate. My childhood was just a series of long days waiting behind bars, like a prisoner. Then later, that little prisoner escaped, trained himself to become strong, and sought to win the championship by participating in a series of barbaric fights. Standing in this corner, I took aim at strangers, taking the initiative to attack. And you, in the other corner, are a passive, weak-willed man, ruled by your father. You're worse off than I am.'

'But I didn't dare to harbour that sadness for long. It's better for a sandbag to not be sad about its function and how weak it is. However, my father didn't want to leave the sandbag in peace, even though it was already a useless empty shell. One fine day, he angrily turned the bag upside down and hung it upside down from a beam.

'At first, I was thoroughly shaken up in that awkward situation. Gradually, I became aware that I was some meaningless object. A meaningless object needed absolutely no awareness of light-headedness or being shaken up.

'Sometimes, I felt like a circus performer. Hanging upside down, dangling from the rafters. I played the game for my father. This unscrupulous audience member knew neither fatigue nor boredom. He sat on the wooden chair below, drinking liquor, laughing hysterically. Occasionally, he swung his whip across my body, as a gesture of appreciation. When I was dizzy and exhausted, unable to bend anymore, he gave me a warning. Punishment, of course, with a whip, accompanied by obscene curse words. My body continued to swing on the beams like a pendulum. He chuckled again. At that time, my only dream was to sprinkle poison on that laughter, or that the rope would break, whereupon I would fall to the ground, break my neck and die. That only thought was like the needle of a wasp, constantly stinging my nerves with venom, making me ache; they nested in me, growing fast, freely proliferating, like a swarm of termites. They gnawed and ate away at all the good thoughts that remained.'

'Scary, huh. If you had got out then, I'm afraid I don't know what would've happened.'

'Yes, every time I paid for an upside-down circus with whiplash, I sharpened my hatred.

'After so many days, I was rescued by a neighbour when he happened to see me unconscious hanging from the rafters. He untied the rope, helped me down, and took me to his house. He brought me warm water to wash the swelling deep in my skin, disinfected the wounds, fed me food, and helped me to sleep. He sat next to me and stroked my back and my hair, lulling me to sleep. In my reverie, I even noticed him leaning down to kiss me. The kiss was like a butterfly fluttering on my forehead. That butterfly always flew into my dreams. I used to wish that it would follow me for the rest of my life.

'So since then, as is the natural course of a person who had been hungry for love for a long time, I often came to him in the hope of having peaceful butterflies on my forehead. Leaning against him, I limped along, learning to raise my head timidly to watch the world light up around me with my eyes half open, my eyelids red and bruised from my father's whips. Over time, I was conquered by him, and then I voluntarily became his adopted son. He helped me sew up the holes in the torn bag. My back was always rubbed, my hair was always stroked, but my soul—he couldn't find anything to fill it with. My soul was an endless pit. He could only hold me in his arms and look at me with sad, confused eyes. When being hugged, just one hug, the world around me suddenly warmed up. A hug was a luxury gift that my father barely gave his poor child; or maybe I didn't deserve it, or maybe it was too much to ask for, or maybe my father didn't realise how important it was. It's also possible that my father viewed hugging as nothing more than a lifeless mechanical movement.

'So my back for many years was often cold. The cold pierced my flesh and froze the bottom of my soul. So that when I received the whips while swinging like a bat hanging from a beam, I didn't know the pain, but only felt the blood falling unconsciously on my pale skin. When that strange neighbour appeared, willing to give me a tight hug, I was unfamiliar with it at first and cowed in self-defence—or perhaps I was afraid. Later, though, I felt a sense of security. I felt the ice in my heart began to melt. I immediately realised that I had just ended a dark life, and at the same time began a new, more unusual one: I became a slave.

'Yes, I'd lost faith in everything, even myself. I was a slave to scepticism; I'm destined to be a slave of scepticism. I thought that hidden behind the noble appearances of my neighbour's love, there must've been some deep thing that I couldn't reveal nor predict.

'I couldn't name what it was.

'I took refuge in him like a larva in a cocoon, relying on him and depending on him for protection, tormented by many cynical questions, like a dog that is often kicked in the hip but still doesn't forget the owner's bowl of rice.

'The rhythm of day and night slowly passed through my life like a scroll, gradually opening and then rolling back in. I became addicted to the pleasure of this strange relationship with a man older than my father, a provocative pleasure mixed with fascination, disgust, and anticipation.

'I know I fell in love with that man.'

93. sling no. 2

'What do you do with those nooses?'

'What did you say, Kan?'

'The creepy nooses in the storeroom, with the bodies dangling, what do you do with them?'

'How do you know, Kan? Did you steal my key?'

'You should answer my question. What do you do with those hideous nooses? Why did you hang them from the rafters?'

'That's my business, my game. I don't want you to meddle with it.'

'Why shouldn't I? They're too creepy. They rolled their eyes at me, asking for help. Those bunch of crooks crawling on the rafters. Like crippled demons. They frighten me to death.'

'Are you really scared? They're just useless.'

'You are crazy. What's the point of tormenting them?'

'Why are you so upset, Kan? They're just mindless dummies, aren't they?'

94. a closed room, a bed of nails, and snakes

There was not much here: down from the ceiling a bayonet-shaped electric bulb glowed with a blue glimmer. On the floor there are squirming swarms of black-and-white snakes, swaying to the music, showing off their forked tongues; and there was a single upholstered bed sprinkled with nails.

G.g was pushed into the room, standing bewildered in front of the door locked from the outside.

The man commanded, 'Lie down on the bed, hurry!' with a low growl in his throat, as if his voice itself had become rusty.

G.g tilted his ear to listen for the noises coming from a small speaker mounted in a secret niche somewhere; he stood facing towards the bed of nails, focused and tense.

'Lie down. Good boy. Try lying down.' The voice softened.

G.g lay down on the bed of nails, his back bouncing and convulsing. The nails gradually collapsed.

'That's good... Now put your feet to the snakes.'

G.g retracted his knees to the point of touching his head, cowering in fear.

'Hurry up! There's not much time left. That's it, fine. Run your feet over the snakes' heads. Again, stronger. Stroking both feet into them. Grab their tongues with your fingers. Yeah, that's great. G.g, you're so good.'

The light bulb went out.

Ah...! In the dense darkness, G.g's scream resounded, as if he were climaxing.

95. the soft bed of nails

'It was one of the games he showed me. We played that game all summer long. The first time, I was really panicking, not knowing what was going on. But then, I quickly found the feeling I've always wanted; every time I fell onto the bed, I knew I was loved and comforted.

'In fact, the nails attached to the bed were made from rubber; they automatically deflated when a heavy force was applied. And the snakes were just rubber snakes. They were like inflated balloons, with one end fastened by a thin thread fixed to the floor. The air movements made them flutter and sway incessantly. A swarm of snakes squirmed in the dim blue light.

'Within the first minute, the threat was calmly neutralised; it was a thrill of ecstasy in agitation. That was what he wanted to give me.'

'Is that all?' Kan asked, staring blankly at the ceiling, his hand still tucked into my chest, gently rubbing my nipples.

'You want to find some meaning in that game? There's no such thing. I've been trying for years to find a meaning, without success. I only know that every time we played that game, we were equal, like two happy kids. We took turns to be locked in the room: sometimes it was him, sometimes it was me. The voice coming from the speaker always changed; I don't remember most of what was said. I remember we talked a lot, about so many things. The door would open when we became tired. We'd walk over to the bed and take off our clothes. He'd pick me up, grab me by the neck, and enter me deep from behind, like a dog. I gritted my teeth because of the pain. I hated how he was so rough; I resented the entire thing, but I didn't know what to do, because I had to be with him. I struggled to expose my immature butt, and he was ashamed of his old body. Occasionally, one of us would shed tears. Little warm drops would drip down my back. I didn't think it was from crying. In fact, it didn't hurt much. Neither was it pleasure. So what was that feeling? All my life I couldn't give a name to it. I only know it was the purest feeling between us. After making love, he would hug me in his arms and sleep soundly on that red bed of nails.

'Once, I woke up in the middle of the night to look for water to drink. I pushed my feet through the cold, slick snakes on the floor and swam through the enveloping darkness. I felt like I no longer existed in real life. Was it heaven or hell? Neither. We belonged to another world, which could've been visible or invisible; an unnamed world that had yet to be recognised, a world that has never existed in any other human being, except for the two of us.

'When we woke up in the early morning fog, we'd often go to the lake near our house to fish. The lake surface was always clear and quiet, as if it had been forgotten from the last century. Flocks of fish leisurely showed off their fins, and silently swam in the water full of green weeds.

'He would bring a dog more than ten years of age, his old best friend. The dog could no longer walk straight; it didn't wag its tail or its ears. It would lazily stretch out on the sun-baked lawn. Clumps of sticky, sparse hair gradually fell off, leaving grey skin spotty with age spots. Sticking out his tongue to breathe, it would look around absently, hardly ever bothering to bark, even when there was an unusual noise behind the canopy of leaves.

'The three of us, one old, one young, one obsolete dog, joined together, forming the three vertices of a flat, empty triangle, like a seed unable to germinate, forgotten in the yard of life.

'We silently set out the baits, occupied with our own thoughts; we didn't know that the strange noise coming from the canopy came from my father.

'He'd been stalking and watching us for a long time, I guess. The dog didn't do his duty. As a result, it had to pay a hefty price.

'Not long after that, I saw the dog lying dead on the steps of my adoptive father's house: it had been beheaded. A savage warning. In order not to hurt him, I quietly took the dog's body and buried it behind the garden under a grove of trees. I carefully wiped the blood stains off the steps with a rag. I thought I would have to come up with a reason, like the dog had gone missing.

'While burying the poor old dog, there arose an irresistible desire in me: the desire to cut off someone's head with a knife. The sunlight melted from above, pouring into my heart like it was casting a block of hot, solid metal.

'However, in that mental state, I didn't have a specific target in mind. Finally, to relieve my frustration, I cut off the head of a cockroach, trampled on a locust, and ripped off the limbs of a green frog that I caught by a small puddle.

'The next time we played the nail bed game, our backs suddenly started bleeding. Someone had replaced the rubber nails with real nails.

'On the floor, among the rubber snakes, there was the corpse of a real snake. Its body had not yet rotten, but the head was smashed, bleeding, sticking out a broken, pathetic tongue.

'Our secret room was no longer a secret.

'Who cruelly disrupted our peaceful life? Who?

'When I woke up one morning a few days later, I found the man next door hanging from the beam above.

'My adoptive father—my lover—was dead.

'On that terrible morning, my father threw me out. He sent me to another city to live with a distant relative.

'I immediately ran away from them. I went to the orphanage myself and took refuge there until I became an adult. I no longer wanted to be connected with any relatives whatsoever. I was on my own.'

'Why did the man next door hang himself?'

'Do you really think he did it himself, or do you think someone did it?'

'...You mean your father, G.g?' Kan's voice trembled.

'I never looked for an answer. To me, it didn't make

much sense. Was it suicide or murder? Was my father the culprit? In the end, the result was the same. He had died, which meant my love died, too. I left that place without ever feeling nostalgic, angry, or sad. I went as far away as possible, as quickly as possible. I left even before my lover's body was taken down by his relatives for burial. I didn't know whether the police came later to investigate, or if the forensic doctor conducted an autopsy. What would they find behind the mysterious death? Would I be arrested for interrogation as a witness, or because of a questionable relationship with the victim, for example? Yet, at that time, I felt empty and lifeless. I felt a little guilty, because he had taken me off the rope and saved my life; now it was up to me, I didn't do the same for him. I owed him a debt I didn't know how to pay.

'Should I have hung myself?

'In any case, I left him. The image that keeps replaying in my head is of someone hanging in the air, as if learning to fly. I believe he was able to fly to heaven, or some distant peaceful realm.

'I remember the last time we slept in that bed of real nails. We splattered with blood, and he said to me, "I love you." In reply, I said, "I love you." In that rare moment, I wasn't sceptical at all.

'Until now, it was the only time in my life that I said—in words—that I loved someone.'

96. the escape

I couldn't run away alone. I needed someone else to help with the hardships in my escape. I went back to find G.g. I was going to take him with me.

Through the hole in the lock, I peeked at him sleeping with Kan in the drawing room. Passionate, infatuated. Both were naked; streaks of colour clung to their arms, back and buttocks. I felt a pang in my heart, but the moment passed unexpectedly quickly. Inside me, I only felt pity for G.g and scorn for Kan—and hatred for both.

I quickly left G.g.'s house. Fine—if he wanted Kan, he could just sit back and wait for the police to come. He should just go to jail alone. I had nothing to do with him.

I whispered goodbye and left.

97. a rendezvous with Kan's ex-lover

I returned to G. world many times. What did I find there but my miserable lust?

Submerged in the blue water, I let the waiter's hand

glide over my back as if it were dancing—scrubbing, grooming, caressing, touching, squeezing.

I didn't remember anyone in this chaotic but silent space. The music, scents, flowing bodies: all were rotting in the depths of the water.

When was the last time I saw G.g drowning in a blue puddle?

When I woke up, I realised that the person lying next to me was that man. That weird masochist guy: Kan's ex-lover.

He was still alone, of course.

We looked silently at each other, peering rudely into the nooks and crannies of the other's flesh, as if turning each body upside down, letting our hidden sick thoughts fall on the tiled floor.

Finally, he said, 'Where's Kan?' with a bossy jerk of the head.

I shyly said, 'I don't know. We have nothing to do with each other anymore.'

'Did he leave you for someone else?' He smirked mockingly.

'I don't care.'

With my face down in the warm water, I suddenly felt

an ache in my lower abdomen. The soles of my feet turned cold. How did I end up in this tragic situation? Honestly, I didn't know whether Kan wanted to stick with me or with G.g. Did I understand Kan at all?

Like a demon from hell, the man was still staring at me inquiringly, and suddenly he burst out laughing. A few people around us raised their heads and stared, frowning.

'I know what happened. That psycho. Did he describe me in detail as a monster? He's very good at making up stories. He turned me into a sickening legend. Baby, I know you're suffering. Has he abandoned you? No! He'll never fully understand the meaning of loving or leaving anyone. He only cares about his own game: setting up a series of tragedies and getting ready to get involved with anyone who looks a bit like him. He traps, he wanders. Isn't life tragic enough?'

The more I listened to him, the more confused I became, like being entangled in a spider's web. What was he saying? Kan made up stories for fun? Kan came to me, made up stories about his ex; but then to G.g, he would make up stories about me—like a monster—to start a new relationship. Then, Kan would abandon G.g. again to make love with someone else? Would G.g also be a victim, like me, like the masochist next to me, or perhaps someone else? The double helix was long and tangled.

Was that Kan's real face? Or was this man slandering Kan, in order to avenge Kan's betrayal?

What was he, actually? I've never been with him. To get to the root of the problem, I ventured to follow him.

Like a deranged man, I followed him home, after only an inviting wink.

I would go to bed with him to find the key to decipher Kan's story. Perhaps I would find out, as I expected, that this man might not be a masochist.

What would I do then? How would I resolve my problem with Kan? And what would happen? Starting a new relationship in such a reckless way?

98. haunted at night

Waking up in the middle of the night, I realised that Kan had left. I found a piece of paper on the refrigerator: 'I'm scared. There were many strange noises in your garden. Some strange shadows were hovering outside the gate. I don't think they're ghosts or hallucinations. Who are they and what are they looking for, G.g?'

The police? I shivered. Through the half-open window, I looked out at the gate. It was quiet; there was nothing strange.

At the end of the garden, where the albino tree was, the foliage swayed slightly. Under the dim moonlight, a small shadow moved lazily. I saw the wolf run across the lawn and disappear into the darkness.

After a while, it suddenly appeared. It bent down to nibble on something and dragged itself on the ground, looking very tired. Then it tried to raise its head. I could see it clearly. It was carrying the copper owl.

A black shadow suddenly emerged from behind the trees, suspiciously small in stature. It looked exactly like the boy whom I had hit a few months ago. Could he have come back to life?

He snatched the owl from the wolf's muzzle, clutching it tightly to his body. The wolf trudged away.

Frightened, I fell to my knees. A light flashed through my mind; I rushed through every room, checked all the door latches, turned off all the lights, and then huddled in the bedroom, holding the largest butcher knife in my hand. I desperately wanted to cry but I couldn't. My whole body was frozen. I wanted to call someone but couldn't find my cell phone. I didn't dare to get out of bed to make long distance phone calls in the living room.

Where's Kan? Where's H? They've left me. Just when I needed them most, they left me to fight alone. Fear turned into hatred. I really hated them.

The arrival of the police at this moment would have been more pleasant than the despair in dealing with that boy's ghost.

How long would it take the devil's hands to open the latch and stand in the middle of the room? Then it would do it—it would take revenge on me by hitting my head with a wooden pestle. That pestle: it was still in the storeroom, which was already locked. I wasn't sure if I had the key. The devil would easily open the storeroom door and find the pestle.

I was fidgeting with the big knife in my hand. How could I kill him again?

99. acquaintances in a strange room

The man told me to take a shower. I snuggled up in the bathroom for a long time. I rubbed soap all over my body, rubbing it over and over until my skin boiled, as if I were trying to peel off my skin. I was extremely nervous.

How many times have I been willing to have sex with a stranger without shame?

If he was as Kan described, what would I do? I looked at the cosmetic products on the shelves: shampoo, shower gel, conditioner, mouthwash, shaving cream, anti-wrinkle cream, sunscreen, lotion, room spray. Then I looked at the clothes rack. A large belt dangled among the messy clothes that Kan had changed into. I immediately thought of the whip.

Just in time, just as I poked my head out of the bathroom, I saw him sitting on the living room lounge chair, talking to some woman. Hearing the sound, she turned around.

Was it her, my comrade?

I froze; I retreated back to the bathroom, threw the towel aside, and put on some clothes. I tried to calm down, took a few deep breaths, looked straight in the mirror, and mustered up the courage to step out.

Why her? What was she doing here?

'This is my sister', the man held out his hand, turning his gaze towards me. I sat down in a chair, facing them. I poured myself a glass of water, and gulped. It'd be great if this were a cup of poison.

She looked at me, her face flat, her eyes empty, and calm, an expression so natural as if she was saying to me, 'It's nothing strange. Nothing surprising. I've known about this for quite some time.'

100. the mask removed

'Have you known my brother for a long time?'

'This is the first time.'

'Where did you meet?'

'A spa.'

'People like you can have comfortable sex after seeing each other for the first time?'

There was silence. I couldn't answer her. I was busy swallowing an invisible seed with a rough shell, trying to push it down my aching throat.

'You think I don't know who you are? No, I just pretended not to know. Let you be natural. If you play tricks in front of me, like pretending to love me, or fool some stupid girl, I will continue to let you be, because I want to study you to see how fake you can be. I will watch you from all sides as if you were a mouse locked in a cage for an experiment, watching you struggle to escape. Thankfully, you're more sincere than I thought. That's why I like you; I hang out with you because I like your professional ability and your not-so-bad thoughts. Other than that, I don't care.

'From the first time I met you, I already knew just by looking deep into the bottom of your eyes when a certain handsome guy passed by; how your fingers would flutter, how you held a glass of water. I know what all of what that signifies. I learned to recognise your world through my brother many years ago.

'When he separated from our family and moved in to a place of his own, I was so disappointed. I was depressed for a long time because I had lost my brother, a close friend who understood me. I resented him. He quietly left me and our family without any explanation; my family became so silent and frustrated. For three years, he disappeared, cutting off most connections. I searched, inquired, and scoured every nook and cranny, hoping to find a satisfactory answer. I even thought he had already killed himself.

'Then one rainy day, I happened to see him come out of a café, hanging out with a friend. They climbed into a taxi, which I secretly followed. He couldn't understand the terrible turmoil in my mind as I stood shivering down the hallway of this apartment building, listening to the steady, cold, melancholy sound of rain in front of the closed door. How many secrets had been hidden from me? My brother suddenly became a stranger. I don't know how many times I was about to knock on the door and ring the bell. But something seemed to be stopping me. And then I wisely returned home in the rain. I stayed up all night thinking: should I tell my parents about this? The next day, I went to find my brother again to talk about it.

'But you know, when we met, the only thing that surprised me was that my brother said that our parents had known he was gay for a long time. They couldn't accept him as he was; they forced him to get married to a woman to return to a "normal" condition. Such a childish thought. Therefore, the optimal solution for him was to get away from the suffocating atmosphere of our family.

'I blame him for not talking openly with me. He said he didn't want to hurt me. But I was hurt anyway.

'From time to time we visited each other. My brother was actually a loner. I never poked my nose into his private love affairs. But I knew that since his long-term boyfriend suddenly moved abroad to settle down, I saw that my brother became more and more lonely. He's had sex with all kinds of people. My brother probably has some kind of masochism. I guess so.'

She stopped and took a sip of water. We watched the river in silence. In the distance, a small boat passed by on the dark water, its lights drilling sharp streaks down into the waves.

Where would the ship go? Is the world as big as people think it is?

101. begging

Hiding behind the door, I heard G.g begging, 'Don't leave me, I beg you! Don't leave me here alone—I'm scared.'

Kan said something, his voice growling decisively, like he was swallowing G.g into his stomach. I saw him throw the tapes on the floor, screaming, 'Look at these damn videos—what did you shoot? You don't stop babbling, doing all kinds of smashing, killing; does it satisfy you? You find pleasure in playing these crazy games, you still want to drag me into it. No, stop. I'm too busy, I'm sane enough to put it aside. I'll throw these in the fire. I'll burn them all.'

G.g knelt on the floor, pleading non-stop. He bent over and picked up the things Kan had thrown away, with a sad, and resigned look. What did he need those for?

A minute later, there was a loud banging on the door. Kan pushed the door open and stepped out. I was shoved into a small gap, crumpled like a gecko behind the door.

Kan slipped into the darkness of the steps, then made his way to the gate. He was carrying a big bag. I knew what was in there. Clothes, laptops, tapes, condoms, lubricants, medicines and aids, douches, cosmetics, razors, etc., all the things that kept him clean, fragrant and shiny.

'You sick, disgusting bastard', I wanted to scream.

Suddenly I loved G.g terribly. Poor G.g. After all, he still needed someone to lean on.

I heard G.g sobbing. He had never shown such extreme weakness.

Kan decided to leave, disappearing behind the iron gate into the dark night. The taxis must've been parked on the main road.

A great mass of hatred welled up in my throat. I wanted to jump up and grab G.g by the nape of his neck, shove his head against the wall, strangle him, throw him in a pan of oil and set him on fire. Damn it! Stop your pitiful whining. Have you lost all self-respect, G.g?

I wanted to run up to Kan and cut his neck with a knife; he was a traitor. I wanted to tie a rope to his feet and hang him upside down on a tall tree branch—or a high voltage pylon—like a stuffed puppet, emotionless and useless. I had a terrible desire to kill. The hot blood circulated and burned in my body.

The wolf came out, rubbing his head against my calves, his eyes widening in bewilderment. I hugged it against my chest. It had grown up. But it was sad. I rarely heard it barking. Maybe it was mute. Or inhibited. All the dogs I've known from my childhood until now have been sad dogs, just like their owners.

The wolf, Kan, the old man next door, the dog of my childhood years, the one that was dumped on the grill, the one whose head was cut off, G.g., and I: we are all stray creatures, outcast and abandoned.

102. break up

Kan stood in front of me and patted me on the shoulder. He announced with a pretence of seriousness (was it real, or was it just my imagination?), 'I'm leaving. I'm going to a new job in another city. My mother and I have moved. The new house is quite large; we can have parties and barbecue in the garden, and we can dance. I don't want to stay here long. Walking around in this city forever is suffocating. I need to end our relationship. I can't keep it up. You've become more and more bizarre, unable to control your behaviour and thoughts. I'm afraid that someone at the company has known about our relationship. Not to mention how you couldn't control yourself at home. I don't want to live in the pain of carrying your body out of the cold bathtub. I don't want to call the police when that happens one day.

'I'm sorry, but you really should stop working for a while. Go to a psychologist or some mental healthcare centre. It will be fine. Take time to solve your problems for good. There was a time when I thought I was in a situation like this. The feeling of dread, the constant quarrels, how you felt like you were deep in the silent darkness with no way out. The cowardly guilt of those who surrendered to fate. And then I lived with it, year after year, for a long time, unable to destroy the hideous evils that grew, expanding, taking root into the viscera, sucking up all the air, spitting out filthy, disgusting faeces.

'At some point in my life, I suddenly became a different person. What was worse, I came to terms with it; I was a shell of a person, controlled by the past that dominated me and would be more ready to throw me in the trash. My life had been bruised. I became a walking dummy, working sanely, but at the bottom of my soul was a dark, empty void. Since you've come, you've pulled me out of this long lull with crazy, endless games. And now it's time for me to leave. I'm grateful to you. Keep in touch. Shall we visit each other from time to time, like best friends?'

Best friends? Two guys who had slept together at night, rode on top of each other, went deep into each other, shared so many things besides bodies and thoughts—how could it be summed up in a simple ending like this?

How could we just be friends?

Kan was gone. Taxi! Taxi! I heard him calling. Streams of traffic glided across the road, sending out sparkling beams of light. The sun shone overhead. What month was it now? Was it spring or summer? I used to teach G.g to how to drown the sun. Yet it still shone overhead, proud, defiant, and eternal. How could I kill a floating object that shines? No one has the power to kill something that shines. Did I fail? Why couldn't I hold onto Kan?

Why do the people I love leave me one by one?

Why are the people in my life all evil?

In the end, nothing has changed. Can't I change anything in my life?

I walked through the busy roadway. My body was cold in the sunlight. I went to the supermarket. I bought a razor, a sledgehammer, a red silk band, a music record, a large green parachute cord, and went home.

Anyway, I still had G.g. at home.

103. final decision

Today is the wolf's one year anniversary. I went to the garden and dug a small hole under the albino tree. The important moment in life has come. When there's nothing left to wait for, we have to end it.

Last night, a stranger claiming to be a neighbour knocked on my door. 'People complain that the noise in your garden keeps them awake. You really should take care of this.'

What? The zombies in the grave came to life. And I had to deal with them. 'What's the matter? Are you a policeman? If not, don't waste your time stalking me. Don't look for those two missing people anymore—I killed them myself. Come on, take me away—put me in jail, torture me, shoot me.'

I never regretted what I did. Killing those two wasn't a crime. In order for them to live, I must die myself. I killed them extremely successfully. And in such a lively way, too. But then they woke up again. Even as ghosts, I always felt that they were too much of a threat: the boy, the old man, the owl. They kept hanging around the edge of the porch, lurking in the dark garden, climbing the albino tree, dangling their legs in the air, swinging around like a merry-go-round. They didn't threaten me, but every now and then they would knock on the door, whispering and squealing. They were just joking around, testing my nerves. They proudly opened the door to the storeroom and rummaged through everything, taking out old photographs, torture devices, the rusted shovel, the rotting wooden pestle, the tattered ropes, and piles of creatures hung dangling. They hung them all from the rafters and buried them all in the albino cemetery.

They thrust deep into me. Way too violently. One by one, they stole things from my life. They sat on the red sofa in the middle of the room, calmly munching on cakes and drinking water. They poured colour into the paintings I had, making them all dirty and ruined.

I wanted to kill them. I tried to kill them.

But I couldn't kill them.

I could only kill the living, not zombies.

Kan left me. H left me. Everyone ran away; they were irresponsible and selfish.

I needed to do something to resolve this. I loved the one-year-old wolf; I would take it with me.

In the end I only had the wolf as a friend.

I covered the wolf's muzzle with a red ribbon and tied its four legs together. It didn't bother to resist as it lay in my arms, whimpering softly. I took it to the bathroom. I heard both of us breathing quietly, tiredly. I threw it in the tub. It lay curled up, motionless. With that docile posture, how much did he love me? I lay down next to it. Both of us wouldn't be alone.

I'd love it forever.

I suddenly realised that I only had the bathroom left.

It was the last refuge for my awakened self. The painted bathroom was riddled with all sorts of weird things. I'd prepared everything—now I will sink deep into the tub and turn on the water.

Looking from the dusty glass window, you could see the joyful leaves hidden in the garden. Outside, the sky was clear and quiet. Lie down, I reassured myself—your time has come.

The music oozed from speakers in the wall. The puffer fish-shaped lamp gave off a halo of jagged spikes. A razor was placed on top of my head. Steam emitted from the water heater.

I was going.

A red halo stretched across the water, seeping into the red silk covering the wolf's muzzle.

104. live

When I returned, the red puddle had erased his helpless face. I stood there looking closely at him. I should have reached in to drag him out.

But in the end, I didn't shake him. I let him die. No regrets.

No regrets.

I went to the garden and used an axe to cut down the albino tree. Then I went upstairs, and smashed the door. I took a look at the old photos. I gathered all the pictures in a pile and put them in a bag. There were many pictures of people so far away, so vague that we couldn't remember who they were, and even if we did remember, we'd never want to see them again. I cut the nooses all over the ceiling. The dolls were slashed, torn and bruised. The puppets were rotting; spiders had made their webs. They all fell with each cut of the string. I also put them in bags.

I buried them all in a large hole in the garden, poured gasoline, and lit a lighter. They burned.

I would return this wooden house to the owner tomorrow. I couldn't remember how many years I'd rented it. From afar, the wooden house looked like a forgotten toy.

In the dark, grey smoke, I heard the indifferent cries of G.g., of the wolf, of the victims I had killed in my life.

Did I regret that G.g was dead?

No. Definitely not.

He, and many others, had to die in order for me to live.

105. fly into the blue lake

I realised that I could fly. I could fly now.

I was flying in the night sky. I would find my world.

I was a flying dummy, like in Magritte's paintings.

I decided to fly high, not throw myself to the ground like Leslie Cheung.

I was flying to the thirteenth floor of the building containing G. world. I wanted to take one last bath and lie down in the lake. Let the magical blue light invade and wash away all the filth and humiliation.

It was the end of my struggle with darkness. I would sink into the deep water. Forever.

106. p

'Don't doubt your imagination, keep interpreting. I encourage inference.

April 1st, do you remember? It was the day that Leslie Cheung ended his life. But his life goes on. He's not dead, at least in my imagination. But also don't forget that it's April 1st.

The whole world knows what day it is.'

THE END

TRANSLATOR'S AFTERWORD

I still remember very well how I felt when I first read *Parallels*. It was a hot summer afternoon in 2009, two years after the novel was first published. I was in my late teenage years then, too young, too curious about myself and my identity, and too eager to explore what the future might hold for me. It was also during this time that I further deepened my passion for literature in general, and queer literature in particular, beyond the syllabus of the first degree I was reading for in politics. It coincided with the first wave of foreign queer literature and films from around the world introduced to a Vietnamese audience, along with works by Vietnamese writers and producers alike.

Among the titles of Vietnamese authors that I voraciously read, and silently judged, *Parallels* stood out as the most unique, and the most brilliantly rendered, because, in addition to its ambitious experiment with form and structure, it is the first literary work written about homosexuals in Vietnam that goes beyond the cliché of characters being sex workers or transvestites. As James Baldwin rightly said, 'You think your pain and your heartbreak are unprecedented in the history of the world, but then you read. You read something which you thought only happened to you, and you discover that it happened 100 years ago to Dostoyevsky.' I could tell myself that when I read *Parallels*, I discovered that what I was struggling with, questions that always lingered in my mind for a long time, might also be what others experienced and questioned on their own. The novel literally changed me and my worldview in so many ways that words seem to fail in their task to do justice in the description of its effects.

Fast forward many years, in the early 2020s, after I had read and edited some representative works in the treasure trove of queer literature, as well as written a master's thesis on queer fiction, I felt an unquenchable urge to re-read *Parallels*. Unapologetic and daring still as it seemed to me at my first reading more than a decade ago; this work, a gem in contemporary Vietnamese literature, deserves to have a wider readership, I have come to believe. And here we are: I would like to bring this translation to you, my dear English-language readers.

Parallels opens with the news about the suicide of Leslie Cheung, a famous Hong Kong actor and singer, a gay icon of Asia. The novel tells the story of life and love revolving three characters: G.g, H, and Kan. *Parallels* also explores complex aspects of lust, BDSM, bestiality, and pederasty. It de-stigmatises mental illness, child abuse, alcoholism, and debunks the conventional view that children are not capable of sexual desire, and thus should be treated as 'sexless creatures.' Violence is ubiquitous in *Parallels*; domestic violence, school bullying, animal cruelty, the violence that returns to incubate another life of violence, as is the solitude that permeates every page. The novel, indeed, dares to tread into dangerous territories that might be unthinkable for many others, and it does so with a generous heart and with masterful skill. Visual and atmospheric, *Parallels* reads somehow like a kaleidoscopic collage, completed yet shattered, *disjecta membra.*

One of the major achievements of *Parallels* is, consequently, its compassionate and somehow obsessive depictions of the victims and perpetrators. This is shown not only in how the outer situations unravel but also through the inner workings of the characters' habits, thoughts, and motivations. Their deep fears and failures are laid bare, without the author's condescension or self-identification with any of them. Moral judgments, hence, remain at the disposal of readers who probably know best how to cast the blame where it truly belongs.

Parallelism lends the novel an idiosyncratic aspect that might make readers feel, in my conjecture, that G.g, H, and Kan are actually the same person. It provides points of views that help us better understand the multi-layered wonderments and intricacies of what it means to be queer within fast-changing circumstances where no role models are available. Furthermore, it puts forwards the idea that in the end, we might find that we are more similar to each other than we think, and that everyone is capable of madness and violence.

Among many others, one question that remains omnipresent throughout *Parallels* is the problem of displacement inasmuch as the ways in which the characters can hardly call anywhere their homes. They are constantly displaced from where they were born, from their parents, from their unaccommodating workplaces, and even from their own queer circles. It must not be coincidental that no clear geographical locations are made that might help readers to locate the setting of the novel. The story told here, technically, can happen anywhere to anyone. Universality, therefore, is one of the effects that the author might inadvertently have produced. The careful, detailed attention that the author pays to portray visceral changes in the characters' bodies as well as their mental perceptions of themselves and the environment around them, moreover, also helps to bring out an uneasy, yet essential feeling, that the displacement and disorientation of their own bodies should hardly be missed.

This translation project would have been unthinkable without the unflinching support and visionary dedication of Kim Trần, the founder and publisher of Major Books. We share a mutual love for this beautiful, though to a certain extent challenging, piece of prose and our commitment to bring more works from Vietnam to the wider world. I owe her a debt of gratitude.

Thanks also go to Samuel Tan, the editor who has done so much to make the text more presentable, who has stood by me with his pen, ink, and sweat, his meticulousness, eyes and mind of an editor that every translator would likely wish they have.

To you, the English-language readers of *Parallels*, I hope you have had an amazing reading experience, and that, perhaps like myself fifteen years ago, you find in the text some questions that you have had yourselves, that perhaps this book might make you feel heard and your solitude more bearable, as the impact it had on me when I was much younger.